Handfasted to the Bear

Reformed Rogues, Volume 2

Elina Emerald

Published by Elina Emerald, 2020.

Table of Contents

Copyright 1
Disclaimer 2
Dedication 3
Chapter 1 – The Beginning 4
Chapter 2 – Present Day 18
Chapter 3 – The Wolf 26
Chapter 4 – Destiny 39
Chapter 5 – The Missive 51
Chapter 6 – Return of the Golden-Hair 59
Chapter 7 – Fools Rush In 70
Chapter 8 – You were Mine 81
Chapter 9 – To Dunsinane 99
Chapter 10 – Macbeth's Castle 108
Chapter 11 – Thorfinn 'the Mighty' Jarl of Orkney 115
Chapter 12 – Brood of Vipers 119
Chapter 13 – The Arrival 134
Chapter 14 – Family Ties 147
Chapter 15 – Wooden Doors 153
Chapter 16 – Two Worlds Collide 158
Chapter 17 - Kiss of Death 170
Chapter 18 – Death Becomes Her 173
Chapter 19 – The Reckoning 186
Epilogue 191
Notes 197

Table of Contents

Copyright 1
Disclaimer 2
Dedication 3
Chapter 1 – The Beginning 4
Chapter 2 – Present Day 18
Chapter 3 – The Wolf 26
Chapter 4 – Destiny 39
Chapter 5 – The Missive 51
Chapter 6 – Return of the Golden-Hair 59
Chapter 7 – Fools Rush In 70
Chapter 8 – You were Mine 81
Chapter 9 – To Dunsinane 99
Chapter 10 – Macbeth's Castle 108
Chapter 11 – Thorfinn 'the Mighty' Jarl of Orkney 115
Chapter 12 – Brood of Vipers 119
Chapter 13 – The Arrival 134
Chapter 14 – Family Ties 147
Chapter 15 – Wooden Doors 153
Chapter 16 – Two Worlds Collide 158
Chapter 17 - Kiss of Death 170
Chapter 18 – Death Becomes Her 173
Chapter 19 – The Reckoning 186
Epilogue 191
Notes 197

Copyright

Copyright ©2020 by **Elina Emerald**
Handfasted to the Bear
Publisher Elina Emerald. All rights reserved. No part of this publication may be reproduced, distributed, or transmitted in any form or by any means, including photocopying, recording, or other electronic or mechanical methods, without the prior written permission of the publisher, except in the case of brief quotations embodied in critical reviews and certain other non-commercial uses permitted by copyright law. For permission requests contact via links below; info@elinaemerald.com or www.elinaemerald.com[1]
Cover design by 100covers

---

1. http://www.elinaemerald.com

Disclaimer

This is a work of FICTION. Although some characters are based on true historical figures and time periods, their depictions are fictitious. Please refrain from pointing out historical inaccuracies found in a made-up love story that happened between two people who never existed. Also, please DO NOT try any of the battle moves at home. I made those moves up using an invisible sword on an imaginary ninja warrior while listening to an 80s mix tape in my kitchen. Which is like playing Hendrix on an air guitar while standing on a fold-out sofa bed. If you play with actual swords, daggers, shotels, and battle-axes you will hurt yourselves. Finally, please do not lock anyone up in a castle dungeon against their will. Outside of a romance novel, it is not a very sociable thing to do and frowned upon in most countries.

Dedication

To my Great Grandaunt, Reapi. A Warrior Queen who raised Warrior Queens. Your legacy lives on.

Chapter 1 – The Beginning

1016 Royal Palace, Lake Hayq, Wollo Province, Abyssinia

Queen Gudit paced the hallways of her palace. Worry and sorrow driving her repetitive behavior. She wore the signatory Habesha *kemis* made of white chiffon with a richly woven *netela* shawl draped across her shoulders.

Despite the simple attire, no one would mistake her for anyone other than the Warrior Queen.

Gudit had reigned sovereign over a vast kingdom for over thirty years and was close to destroying an Axumite empire twice the size of her own.

To her detractors, she was a ruthless usurper, a rebel. To her supporters, she was a legitimate ruler from a dynastic family.

Whatever the preconceptions, none could deny she was born to lead, and she did with fire and military acumen.

But the Queen was foremost a mother who cherished her children. Losing her youngest daughter, the thing she mourned the most. At twenty-one, Izara had vanished after traveling to *Yemnat*. Months of searching had proved futile... until now.

Gudit's pacing ceased when Zenabu, her trusted advisor, approached. He bowed in reverence before saying, "My *Nigisiti*, I have received word from Ajani."

Zenabu ushered the messenger forward. He was a young, attractive man, dark-skinned with the lean physique of a runner who could cover long distances without rest.

"Speak," Gudit said in an authoritative voice.

The messenger bowed. "Master Ajani says *Li'iliti* Izara was captured from the *Port of Zeila* by Norsemen."

Gudit turned to Zenabu. "What is these Norsemen?"

"They are white, golden-haired raiders from a land called Norway," he replied.

The Queen whipped her head back to the messenger. "Continue."

"The *li'iliti* was seized as a gift for their king. A man called Ol... af Harald... sson."

"Ol... af? What kind of name is this? What are his demands?"

"He made no demands, my *Nigisiti*. She was to become one of his thralls."

Gudit tried to school her features, but her rage got the better of her. She shouted, "Do you mean to tell me my daughter, a descendant from a thousand, year-old dynasty is to become the *slave* of some... Olaf?"

Gudit threw the cup of wine she was holding at the wall. It narrowly missed the messenger's head.

The messenger replied, "Yes, my *Nigisiti*."

"What do you mean *was*? What are you not telling me?" Her hand shot out, grabbing him by the throat with the intent to squeeze.

Zenabu intervened before the Queen lost all composure. He dismissed the relieved messenger and explained the rest. "It seems the *li'iliti* never arrived in Norway. Her captor..." He hesitated.

"Her captor did what?" The Queen tensed, knowing that if her daughter were dead, she would reign fire upon these Norsemen.

Zenabu cleared his throat. "Her captor took her with him. He did not return to his king."

The Queen visibly relaxed before confusion marred her features. "Then where did he take her?"

"He took her to a foreign land surrounded by the sea. They call it... Orkney."

1018 Birsay, Orkney Isles

IZARA MEZMER WATCHED the raging sea from the castle wall-walk. Her raven black hair and iridescent dark skin glistened in the wintery sunlight. The signatory robes marking her as a thrall billowed as the icy winds lashed the material across her protruding belly.

She was thousands of miles from her beloved homeland, staring at the vast expanse of ocean. She was in a foreign landscape as striking and terrifying as the Norse Jarl who had captured her on a Viking raid.

"Git inside, it's cold." A deep voice rumbled from behind her before she felt a fur-lined coat being draped across her shoulders.

Izara turned towards her captor.

He was a fearsome-looking man with a firm jawline and rugged facial features. Fair skin with a head of thick black unruly hair. He looked so different from the other golden-haired Vikings, yet to her, he was striking. He towered above her. Violence and brutality pulsed from his very being. None of it had ever touched her.

She had witnessed his rage unleashed upon others if they dared to cross him. But to her, he was always a protective lover with an abundance of kindness... but only to her.

"I just needed air," she said with a reassuring smile.

"Whitna' bout the bairn?"

"The bairn is fine."

"Did ye have another vision?" he asked.

"It was nothing." She lied.

His worried eyes assessed her as he frowned.

Izara furrowed her brow in return. It was a look she gave him when she was trying to read his mood.

Zenabu ushered the messenger forward. He was a young, attractive man, dark-skinned with the lean physique of a runner who could cover long distances without rest.

"Speak," Gudit said in an authoritative voice.

The messenger bowed. "Master Ajani says *Li'iliti* Izara was captured from the *Port of Zeila* by Norsemen."

Gudit turned to Zenabu. "What is these Norsemen?"

"They are white, golden-haired raiders from a land called Norway," he replied.

The Queen whipped her head back to the messenger. "Continue."

"The *li'iliti* was seized as a gift for their king. A man called Ol... af Harald... sson."

"Ol... af? What kind of name is this? What are his demands?"

"He made no demands, my *Nigisiti*. She was to become one of his thralls."

Gudit tried to school her features, but her rage got the better of her. She shouted, "Do you mean to tell me my daughter, a descendant from a thousand, year-old dynasty is to become the *slave* of some... Olaf?"

Gudit threw the cup of wine she was holding at the wall. It narrowly missed the messenger's head.

The messenger replied, "Yes, my *Nigisiti*."

"What do you mean *was*? What are you not telling me?" Her hand shot out, grabbing him by the throat with the intent to squeeze.

Zenabu intervened before the Queen lost all composure. He dismissed the relieved messenger and explained the rest. "It seems the *li'iliti* never arrived in Norway. Her captor..." He hesitated.

"Her captor did what?" The Queen tensed, knowing that if her daughter were dead, she would reign fire upon these Norsemen.

Zenabu cleared his throat. "Her captor took her with him. He did not return to his king."

The Queen visibly relaxed before confusion marred her features. "Then where did he take her?"

"He took her to a foreign land surrounded by the sea. They call it... *Orkney*."

1018 Birsay, Orkney Isles

IZARA MEZMER WATCHED the raging sea from the castle wall-walk. Her raven black hair and iridescent dark skin glistened in the wintery sunlight. The signatory robes marking her as a thrall billowed as the icy winds lashed the material across her protruding belly.

She was thousands of miles from her beloved homeland, staring at the vast expanse of ocean. She was in a foreign landscape as striking and terrifying as the Norse Jarl who had captured her on a Viking raid.

"Git inside, it's cold." A deep voice rumbled from behind her before she felt a fur-lined coat being draped across her shoulders.

Izara turned towards her captor.

He was a fearsome-looking man with a firm jawline and rugged facial features. Fair skin with a head of thick black unruly hair. He looked so different from the other golden-haired Vikings, yet to her, he was striking. He towered above her. Violence and brutality pulsed from his very being. None of it had ever touched her.

She had witnessed his rage unleashed upon others if they dared to cross him. But to her, he was always a protective lover with an abundance of kindness... but only to her.

"I just needed air," she said with a reassuring smile.

"Whitna' bout the bairn?"

"The bairn is fine."

"Did ye have another vision?" he asked.

"It was nothing." She lied.

His worried eyes assessed her as he frowned.

Izara furrowed her brow in return. It was a look she gave him when she was trying to read his mood.

His eyes softened before he gathered her into his arms. Her back to his front, one hand gently caressing her stomach, cradling their unborn child.

"I mis return to Caithness in the morn. There is trouble brewing with my half-brothers. Ah'll need to go to Norway to petition King Olaf about their territories."

"Should I come with you?" Izara set her troubled eyes on him.

"No love, ye are safest here. But I promise ah'll return in time to meet our bairn."

Izara relaxed once again into his warm, comforting embrace as they stared at the Atlantic Ocean in silence.

Clutching the rosary beads in her hand, she uttered a silent prayer that her premonition was false. But deep down inside, she knew she would not live long enough to watch their child grow.

1023 Lerwick, Shetland Islands

THE WIND PICKED UP its pace as five-year-old Orla curled up in her warm bed. She had been through many upheavals in her brief life. Abandoned at birth, she had moved from one household to another. Always hidden away.

Orla learned to adapt and adjust to any circumstance, but no matter how much she tried, she could not shake the loneliness of being an orphan and having no last name to speak of.

Startled by a sound, she opened her eyes to see Runa; the woman caring for her.

"Wake up, peedie bird. Ye're aboot to go on a journey."

"Where to?" Orla asked in a loud voice.

"Shh quiet, no one must ken ye are leaving." A familiar voice spoke behind her.

It was Hagan, Runa's husband. Orla had been living with the couple and their son, Torstein, for some time.

Hagan was already gathering her things together while Runa started dressing Orla in warm clothes.

In hushed tones, Orla asked, "Can I take Mira?"

"No, lass, ye cannot take yer puppy. He will make much noise," Hagan replied.

"Whitna' bout Tor, can he come?"

"No, he is still away at sea," Runa said, hugging her.

Orla hugged her back but looked confused when Runa started wiping tears from her eyes.

"Why are you weeping, Runa?"

"Because ah'll miss ye. Now mind on yer prayers daily and try to keep out of trouble."

Orla nodded.

Then Hagan crouched down beside her. "Remember the silent game we played when ye were a bairn?" Hagan asked.

"Aye."

"We *mis* play it again now, sweeting." He stretched out his hand towards her.

Orla placed her tiny hand in his big, calloused one and followed him through the darkened tunnels below the homestead that led to the ocean.

When they arrived at the opening, Orla saw a longboat on the shore with men on board.

Hagan picked her up, his loosened blonde hair flying behind him as he ran towards the sea.

"Where are we, gan?" Orla asked, holding on tight as they moved faster.

"To Scotland."

"Why?"

"We *mis* hide ye again, lass."

"Hide me? Who from?"
"A monster."

※

1024 MacGregor Land, Glenorchy

The Bear

ORLA HATED SCOTLAND. The children were mean because she looked different and talked strangely. They laughed and poked fun at her hair, her skin color, her clothes.

Because she did not know who her parents were, they also called her, 'Orla the Orphan.' That slur hurt the most. To be reminded daily that she had no last name, and no kin, was like pouring salt on a festering wound.

The kids also teased her because she lived with Morag 'the Oracle.' Although Morag looked scary with her long white hair and eerie eyes, Orla felt a powerful bond with her.

She tried not to cry when the others said mean things, but she was only six summers old, and everything about the place and its people was strange to her.

When the taunts became too much, Orla would run into the woods and sit near a large rowan tree. Its branches, she imagined, were the arms of a loving parent reaching out to console her as she sheltered in its embrace.

On one particularly bad day, feeling so alone, Orla was sobbing by the tree when a large boy stepped out from behind it. At first, she was terrified, thinking he meant her harm, but he told her not to be afraid. He just needed to sit and rest a while in the shade.

Orla noticed he had cuts on his arms and when he turned his face fully to her, she gasped to see one side swollen and bruised.

"Are you all right?" Orla asked tentatively as he winced when he sat down beside her.

"Aye... just a wee bit sore tis all."

"What happened to you?"

"I... fell off a horse."

They sat in silence for a while until he asked, "Why are ye crying, lass?"

"The children here are very mean."

He nodded in understanding, then told her he came to the tree too sometimes when people made him sad.

They talked for a long time about many things, and soon Orla realized she did not feel so alone anymore because that day she made her first real friend. His name was 'Brodie Fletcher' and because of his size, they called him 'the Bear'. He became her protector.

From then on, whenever the village children teased her, Brodie would threaten them, and they would stop. Brodie even let her go hunting with him sometimes.

Orla decided she wanted to be a hunter, just like him.

Brodie introduced Orla to his friend. A boy named 'Beiste'. He was the MacGregor chieftain's son, and he was kind to her. Beiste became her second friend.

1026 Handfasted

WHEN ORLA WAS EIGHT years old and Brodie twelve, he told her he and Beiste were leaving to foster with the Murrays. They would be gone a long while.

Orla ran to her rowan tree, weeping because she would miss Brodie. He was her one loyal friend. He had been there for her when she had no one, and she had kept him company when his father hurt him. Over the years, Brodie's father hurt him a lot.

"What's wrong, Orla? Dinnae cry. I'll return someday," Brodie said when he found her by their tree.

"Brodie, you are my one true friend. What if you never come back? I will be alone forever." Orla sobbed.

"You'll not be alone forever. There'll be many men trying to court you, for you're a bonnie catch."

"Not when I am different."

"Och, when I return, you'll be married to a handsome man. But none as braw as me you ken." He winked at her to break the somber mood.

"No one will marry me, Brodie."

"Dinnae say that, Orla."

"Tis true."

"Well, how about we agree that if no one marries you, I will?"

"Really? You promise?"

"Aye. I do. Here, we can use my hair tie to create a handfast." He held her hand and released the leather tie that bound his long hair. He then tied it around their wrists, securing it in a knot.

"What does it mean?" Orla asked.

"My aunt says tis what couples do if they want to be together but are not ready for marriage."

"All right, let's hand... past?"

"Handfast Orla. With our hands together bound fast like this." He lifted their entwined hands.

"Now what?" she asked.

"Well, there are always words spoken." He cleared his throat. "I, Brodie the Bear, take you, Orla, as my wife if no one marries you." Brodie nudged her. "Now you say it."

"I Orla the Orphan..." She paused awkwardly.

Brodie interrupted and shook his head. "No, Orla. Dinnae call yourself that. How about... Orla the... Huntress?"

Orla nodded and smiled. "I, Orla, the Huntress takes you, Brodie, as my husband, in case no one marries me."

"Done. Feel better now?"

"Aye, Brodie. Thank you." Orla beamed at him.

"Och, tis alright, lass. Here, you take the tie and keep it as a reminder." Brodie untied their hands, giving her the leather tie to hold.

"Will you come and say goodbye to me before you leave, Brodie?"

"Of course, we're handfasted." He winked at her.

Owen Fletcher

AFTER LEAVING ORLA by the tree, Brodie realized the time was late and sprinted home. He could see a storm approaching, and he still had chores to complete before dark. His dad was easily angered, so he ran with trepidation. If he snuck in through the barn, he would be safe.

As he rounded the fence line, fear gripped him. His father, Owen, was standing beside the barn. Brodie could tell he was well into his cups, and the look on his face promised retribution.

Owen Fletcher was a goliath of a man with heavy-set arms and enormous fists. Fists he had no compunction unleashing when inebriated. The force of his swing could cripple a grown man, but to a boy half his size, the carnage was devastating. It was pure luck he had not killed his son in one of his rages. That luck was about to run out and Brodie knew it.

Brodie knew he was courting trouble when he saw the strap his father was holding, and from his angry demeanor, he was livid.

"Weil, where ha ye been? Yer chores are not done." Owen sneered.

"I've been training with the lads."

"Dinnae lie to me. Ye've been sniffing around that black-moir orphan."

"What's wrong, Orla? Dinnae cry. I'll return someday," Brodie said when he found her by their tree.

"Brodie, you are my one true friend. What if you never come back? I will be alone forever." Orla sobbed.

"You'll not be alone forever. There'll be many men trying to court you, for you're a bonnie catch."

"Not when I am different."

"Och, when I return, you'll be married to a handsome man. But none as braw as me you ken." He winked at her to break the somber mood.

"No one will marry me, Brodie."

"Dinnae say that, Orla."

"Tis true."

"Well, how about we agree that if no one marries you, I will?"

"Really? You promise?"

"Aye. I do. Here, we can use my hair tie to create a handfast." He held her hand and released the leather tie that bound his long hair. He then tied it around their wrists, securing it in a knot.

"What does it mean?" Orla asked.

"My aunt says tis what couples do if they want to be together but are not ready for marriage."

"All right, let's hand... past?"

"Handfast Orla. With our hands together bound fast like this." He lifted their entwined hands.

"Now what?" she asked.

"Well, there are always words spoken." He cleared his throat. "I, Brodie the Bear, take you, Orla, as my wife if no one marries you." Brodie nudged her. "Now you say it."

"I Orla the Orphan..." She paused awkwardly.

Brodie interrupted and shook his head. "No, Orla. Dinnae call yourself that. How about... Orla the... Huntress?"

Orla nodded and smiled. "I, Orla, the Huntress takes you, Brodie, as my husband, in case no one marries me."

"Done. Feel better now?"

"Aye, Brodie. Thank you." Orla beamed at him.

"Och, tis alright, lass. Here, you take the tie and keep it as a reminder." Brodie untied their hands, giving her the leather tie to hold.

"Will you come and say goodbye to me before you leave, Brodie?"

"Of course, we're handfasted." He winked at her.

Owen Fletcher

AFTER LEAVING ORLA by the tree, Brodie realized the time was late and sprinted home. He could see a storm approaching, and he still had chores to complete before dark. His dad was easily angered, so he ran with trepidation. If he snuck in through the barn, he would be safe.

As he rounded the fence line, fear gripped him. His father, Owen, was standing beside the barn. Brodie could tell he was well into his cups, and the look on his face promised retribution.

Owen Fletcher was a goliath of a man with heavy-set arms and enormous fists. Fists he had no compunction unleashing when inebriated. The force of his swing could cripple a grown man, but to a boy half his size, the carnage was devastating. It was pure luck he had not killed his son in one of his rages. That luck was about to run out and Brodie knew it.

Brodie knew he was courting trouble when he saw the strap his father was holding, and from his angry demeanor, he was livid.

"Weil, where ha ye been? Yer chores are not done." Owen sneered.

"I've been training with the lads."

"Dinnae lie to me. Ye've been sniffing around that black-moir orphan."

Brodie clenched his fists, and his entire body stiffened. He did not like anyone aiming slurs at Orla.

"No, I was training."

Without warning, Owen backhanded Brodie across the face. Then followed it with a hard punch to his stomach.

Brodie buckled and fell to his knees, winded.

"Ye stay away from her. She's cursed like that *Cailleach* witch, Morag."

"She's just a lass Da."

"A Viking whore's bastard, that's what she is and ye'll not taint our bloodline with the likes of her."

Brodie blocked his father's strap from hitting him in the face.

That only angered Owen more.

"Muriel saw ye in the woods, said ye was handfasting with that orphan." His father spat on the ground like even thinking about her was abhorrent.

"Twas nothing." Brodie could hear the panic in his voice.

His father dropped the strap and deferred to his weapon of choice. His fists. He began cursing and swinging. Beating his only son in between drunken slurs. "Women will ruin ye. Remember that."

"Aye Da—"

"They make ye weak. Dinnae let them control ye." Owen beat Brodie with vigor.

"Never love a lass. She will rip your balls asunder!" His father was yelling now and kicking Brodie in the ribs.

Brodie knew to take the beatings. To resist was akin to suicide. He curled himself into a tight ball and prayed it would be over soon.

"Dinnae fall in love ever, ye hear me?" Owen ranted.

"Aye," Brodie mumbled as the heavens burst open with icy rain.

Brodie cowered in the wet mud. Beaten and bruised, he tried hard not to cry as his father then launched into kicking his back.

Brodie saw Orla staring at him through the trees. *What was she doing here?* He saw her pick up a large rock and move towards his father. Brodie's heart lurched. At that moment, he cared nothing for his safety but only to protect her.

He could not let her come closer. She would get hurt. Brodie realized then Orla was his weakness. He had placed her in danger. His father was right, women made you weak.

Brodie shouted, "No. *Orphan*... go home!"

Orla paused, looking stricken at the term. She moved closer when he yelled, "Go home, *Orphan*, ye dinnae belong here!"

Then she fled.

After what felt like an eternity of hell, Brodie could barely see through his swollen eyes. Feeling like he was drifting in and out of consciousness, he heard a roar, and then his father was thrown backward and landed on his backside in the mud.

Chieftain Colban MacGregor stood over Brodie protectively. "Enough, Owen. Your son has had enough." Colban MacGregor was a menacing man, and if anyone could gainsay Owen Fletcher, it was the chieftain.

"This does not concern ye. My boy needs to be taught a lesson or he will become weak like his ma."

"Your wife was ne're weak, Owen," Colban said.

"My wife was a harlot who left me for another man," Owen yelled.

"Your wife left ye because ye are a drunkard who beats women and defenseless boys."

Owen got to his feet and ran straight at Colban, hellbent on knocking him down. But what Owen failed to realize was the MacGregor chieftain was not a defenseless twelve-year-old boy. He was a grown man, a skilled warrior, and a vicious opponent.

Colban maintained his protective stance over Brodie, providing shelter from the storm. He braced and took the full impact of Owen's body weight. Then he used that momentum to spin Owen around just enough so he could grip his neck in a firm chokehold.

Brodie could just make out his father struggling to loosen the arm bound around his neck. His face was going red, then blue, until he passed out from lack of oxygen. Only then did Colban release him.

Brodie watched as the chieftain threw his father's unconscious body onto the ground and called Beiste.

"Son, take Brodie to the Keep while I deal with this sorry excuse of a man."

Brodie saw Beiste appear in his line of vision. His humiliation was complete. He was ashamed, his best friend had witnessed such a pitiful display.

Beiste leaned forward and carefully helped Brodie to his feet, taking most of Brodie's weight as they walked. When they passed Brodie's father, Beiste spat on the ground where he lay. "I mean no disrespect, Brodie, but your da is a coward. Tis lucky he didn't kill you."

Brodie felt dazed. Blood was streaming down his face from lacerations and cuts as he tried to breathe through broken ribs. He had to admit, after all the years of abuse he had endured, this was by far the worst.

Then Beiste said, "If twas not for Orla calling for help, he might have done just that."

Brodie just grunted. He was in too much pain to do anything else.

The next day, Brodie and Beiste went away to foster with the Murrays where they would train to become warriors. Brodie did not look back. The chieftain had saved him from certain death, and he would make the Clan proud. He no longer had any room in his heart for weakness of any kind.

Orla waited by the rowan tree for hours, hoping Brodie would meet her to say goodbye.

He never did.

1035 The Return

BRODIE RETURNED NINE years later with a large procession of MacGregor warriors. A wildly handsome man, he was almost unrecognizable. He was open and affable, but there was a hard edge to him. Underneath the charm and carefree demeanor lay a simmering rage.

The entire Keep had been in a frenzy of excitement to prepare for their return. Women were primping themselves, hoping to catch a warrior's eye, and families were awaiting a reunion with their sons.

Orla was now seventeen, and she was eager to welcome Brodie home. She thought of him many times over the years and hoped they would have time to talk. She wanted to show him the bows and arrows she had fashioned and catch him up on village news.

Orla had worn her best dress and tied back her curly hair using the handfast leather tie.

When Brodie rode past, Orla called out his name and waved. He looked stunned when he saw her, then a shuttered expression came over him. He gave her a brief nod and continued riding.

Orla followed behind, wondering if maybe he did not recognize her. Maybe he had forgotten her.

When the warriors reached the Keep, Orla hovered close by, hoping for another opportunity to speak to Brodie. It never came.

Brodie dismounted his horse inundated with female admirers. Orla watched as he took the hand of a woman named Saundra and they disappeared into the woods together. She saw them kiss, and her heart shattered for some unknown reason.

That summer she watched Brodie go into the woods with a long succession of different women. One replaced another and another. Worse was the realization that this Brodie was a stranger to her. The old Brodie had died, replaced by a colder version.

One sunny day Orla sat under her rowan tree mourning the loss of her old friend. She stared at the horizon, lost in thought.

"Orla, why so sad?"

It startled her to see Brodie casually leaning against the tree. She quickly wiped her tears away and feigned a smile. A rebellious part of her was happy he had sought her company, like old times. Her joy was short-lived however when she heard a woman giggle behind him. Brodie looked irritated, but it was enough for Orla to realize he had arranged a tryst with one of his women at their tree. *Their tree.*

Brodie raised an eyebrow at Orla, challenging her to say something. Orla just shook her head in disgust and walked away without a word. She knew then, the Bear who protected her was no more. He had left a long time ago and never returned. No one ever returned for her.

That afternoon Orla walked to the rocky outcrop above the Training Grounds. She pulled the handfast leather tie from her hair and threw it over the edge.

After that summer, Orla never returned to the rowan tree again. Her place of solace forever tarnished. She also refused to pay Brodie Fletcher any more attention going to great lengths to avoid him. Orla's heart would remain closed off where he was concerned.

Chapter 2 – Present Day

1042 Kirkwall, Orkney

"*Far*, Open up!" Torstein Hagansson pounded on the door of his parents' cottage.

"Whit, is it, son?" Hagan Alfsson ushered Torstein inside and barred the door behind him.

"Orla's in danger."

Runa, his mother, emerged from the bedchamber in her nightgown. "Whits happened?"

"Rognvald has returned. He kens she's alive," Torstein replied.

The blood drained from Runa's face. "But hoo?"

"He found letters from Brusi to Einar. He doesn't want the jarl to discover her existence."

Runa collapsed into a chair and said, "Ye have to git Orla now."

"I leave for Glenorchy tonight with my men. I only came to warn ye." Torstein turned to his father. "Take *Mor* away from here. It willna be long afore they come for ye both."

"We'll leave at once. But son..." Hagan grabbed Torstein's shoulders in a firm grip. "Take her to Dunsinane. Macbeth will ken what to do."

"Why would the Scottish king ken what to do?"

"He's her kin and the only one who can find the jarl."

Torstein stared at his father as the missing pieces fell into place. He knew then he had to move fast.

MacGregor Woodlands, Glenorchy

Brodie

AT TWENTY-EIGHT YEARS of age, Brodie Fletcher was a heartbreaking rogue. Ever since he was old enough to seduce women, he had led a life of lasciviousness and an overindulgence of sexual pleasure. That was all it was, physical pleasure. He made no emotional attachments, and the women he invited into his bed were of a similar mindset.

His one drawback was he could never remember their names. Before, during, or after his carnal relations. But he made sure he satisfied his bed partners, which is why a night with Brodie elicited a night of wanton pleasure for the women involved.

As his prowess in the bedchamber became legendary, women sought him out.

For years, he had accepted a simple life of sensual pursuits. But in the past two summers, he noticed a gradual change in his sexual proclivities.

They became non-existent.

His interest in women had waned to the point he found abstinence more pleasurable than seduction. Judging by the disastrous night he had just spent with Helda. *Or was it Zelda?* When he could not summon enough passion to even become aroused, Brodie took this as a clear sign he was undergoing some strange metamorphoses.

It all came down to one woman. *Orla.*

The only female who looked at him with disdain and contempt. Theirs was a tenuous relationship at best. At worst, it was outright hostile. Brodie knew if he were on fire, Orla would set up camp around him and roast a wild boar over the flames.

Yet he could not stay away.

Which is why Brodie was currently stalking Orla through the woods. It was not an effortless task, given how fast the vixen could run. He was practically out of breath half the time. But the exhilaration of the chase made him feel alive.

It was always that way with her.

Even when they were arguing, and her barbs were shredding his fragile ego, he felt energized. She was the only woman who could get under his skin and tear out his sinews. She was *that*... irritating... and utterly captivating.

Brodie had known from childhood Orla was special. At eight, she ran circles around him. At seventeen, she had the power to bring him to his knees. And now... she was a formidable force of sheer beauty.

Brodie kept himself hidden in the dense woodlands and watched as Orla stopped near a tree. She crouched down, her bow and quiver strapped to her back. Orla pulled out a dirk from her boot and made a scuff mark on the tree close to its roots. She touched the dirt, closed her eyes, took a deep breath, then opened them. She stood and started running again. Brodie wondered who or what she was tracking.

He kept pace with her from a short distance away. He thought it ironic that the *'Huntress'* was being stalked by the *'Bear'*.

He watched as Orla came to a clearing and slowed to a walk. He heard her muttering and cursing to herself.

Brodie was trying to make out what she was saying when something caught his eye in the distance. Someone was standing in the shadows. Brodie saw a flash of flint. His feet were already moving as he sprinted straight towards Orla. His heart pounding with panic. He prayed he reached her in time.

Orla

ORLA WAS CALLED MANY names over the years. Orla black moir, Orla the bastard, Orla the orphan. Some snickered and uttered insults to her back, jealous she had risen to such a high position within the Clan. While others were more forthcoming with their insults. Whatever the name, she had learned to ignore it, hold her head high and work hard.

That hard work paid off as she earned the respect and friendship of many in the Clan.

Orla was a skilled bowyer fashioning weapons for some archers who did not mind a female crafting their bows. She was also a close confidante and advisor to Amelia MacGregor, the chieftain's wife.

From the moment they met, they were kindred spirits, and nothing had changed. Except, Amelia was now a mother of two precious bairns who the fearsome chieftain, Beiste MacGregor, doted on. It was heartwarming to watch how much love the once cold-hearted 'Beast' held for his wife and bairns.

As Amelia's advisor, Orla was constantly in the Keep attending to matters regarding the chieftain's family. And there lay the problem. Anything regarding their safety also involved Brodie Fletcher.

As Beiste's Head Guardsman, Brodie was a constant thorn in Orla's side. He overrode her decisions, interfered with her events, questioned her whereabouts, and often shadowed her if she went to the village.

If he were in a surly mood, they would bicker over every little thing. Their arguments would end in a shouting match where Brodie inevitably calls her an 'orphan' before she stormed off. Now, they were arch enemies, and Orla was tempted to shoot his ass with an arrow the next time they crossed paths.

"Turd... swine... coos dung!" Orla cursed to herself as she stomped through the woods in pitch darkness. Annoyed with that infuriating man.

Of all the nights for her to patrol the woods, she had to stumble across him, sneaking out of Zelda's cottage half-naked and wreaking of cheap perfume. *Ugh!*

Orla cringed at the unwarranted pain that the image slashed across her mind. Then she tamped it down. *What did she care who he cavorted with?* There were far more important things to be concerned about, like Norse invaders making their way across Scotland.

Orla needed to concentrate and do her part to maintain the safety of Clan MacGregor. *Vigilance.* She had to stop thinking about that man-whore.

Caught up in her musings, Orla had stopped paying attention to her surroundings until she heard a twig snap.

In the silence of the woods, it could herald a wild animal or something sinister. She stilled, held her breath, and looked in the sound's direction. She remained quiet, a hand resting on the hilt of her dagger. Her heightened senses were on alert.

Then she heard it. A low keening sound slicing through the air followed by an urgent whisper, "Orla, get down!"

She turned in time to catch an enormous shadow looming over her before she tumbled to the ground. A split second later, an arrow embedded itself in the tree behind her.

Orla stared in shock at the arrow, then stared directly into the face of *Brodie... bloody.... Fletcher!* Her body pinned beneath his.

"What–"

Brodie's large hand clamped over her mouth. "Be quiet."

Orla yanked her head away from his hand. "Get off me. You reek of stale flowers." She hissed. Brodie glared at her before they both heard footsteps approaching and movement in the distance.

They froze, their bodies melded together, quietly breathing as one. She could hear voices, two men talking.

"I ken she's dead. I heard something fall over there."

"Aye, Vidar, yer arrows rarely miss."

Orla felt Brodie's body tense at their words as he was scanning the woods. In a fast but silent sequence of moves, Brodie stood and lifted her into a standing position. "We go now."

He picked her up as if she weighed nothing and started running towards a large boulder. He set her down once they reached it and shoved her behind him. "Quiet. I need to see who they are," he said. Then dismissed her and stared out into the night.

Orla glared daggers at his back. It was so typical of Brodie to run roughshod over her. If the situation were not so dire, she would have smacked him on the back of the head. It was while she was glaring at his broad, muscular shoulders that she realized two things. First, someone named 'Vidar' had tried to kill her, and second, Brodie just saved her life.

Brodie

BRODIE'S HEART WAS pounding, adrenalin coursing through his bloodstream. He was livid and trying to decipher what was happening. All he knew was some cur just tried to shoot Orla. *But why?* He could not fathom it, neither did he have time to relive the feeling of pure fear when he thought she was in danger. He shuddered to think what would have happened if he had not followed her tonight.

As his mind drew upon several scenarios, the most pressing was finding out what these men were about, and the second was never letting Orla out of his sight again. The woman was a beacon for trouble.

The men came closer. Brodie clutched the hilt of his sword. They came to the spot where the arrow was lodged.

"Looks like ye missed Vidar."

"But I heard someone fall doon here."

"We must find her, or the earl will kill us instead."

The men stepped out of the shadows; Brodie saw them for the first time. He recognized neither of them. Their manner of speech was also strange. They were not part of the MacGregor clan. He wondered why the sentinels in the trees had not alerted them to the danger.

As the men approached, Brodie had a plan of attack. It would be fast and simple. Jump out, knock them unconscious, take them back to the Keep for questioning.

He was about to move forward when an arrow flew from behind him, hitting one man in the neck, killing him instantly. The remaining man was startled and ran. Brodie cursed and turned to see Orla nocking a second arrow on the bowstring and taking aim.

He deflected her shot. "No! We need him alive for questioning." He ran in pursuit of the second man.

Orla started running alongside him.

"Get back behind the boulder now," he shouted at her.

"I'm faster, I'll catch him," Orla said as she sprinted past Brodie.

"Orla, no!" Brodie was trying to stop her, but it was too late she had already veered to the right to head off the assailant and was standing directly in front of him braced to tackle him head-on. But Brodie beat her to it and took him down from behind. The man hit the dirt so hard he knocked himself out.

Brodie stood up and stormed over to Orla. "What the bloody hell was that? I told you to stay behind me," he roared.

"I was trying to help. I almost stopped him."

"How? By placing your body in front of a man who just tried to kill you. Why didn't you hand him your dagger and say, 'Here I am, just stab me right in the chest.' Maybe that would have stopped him." Brodie made a hand gesture of an invisible knife stabbing his chest.

Orla was about to lash out when she realized she had just placed herself in a prime position to be killed. "Ooh," she replied, looking contrite.

"I swear if you ever do that again I'll take a strap to your backside and tie you to my bed for a week!" Brodie yelled.

Orla just blushed then looked indignant.

Brodie stomped back over to the unconscious man, hefted him over his shoulder, and started walking back to the Keep. "We need to notify the others. I'll send men to scour the woods and collect the body."

They walked in silence for some time before Orla said, "Just so you ken, I didn't mean to kill that man. I just wanted to stop him from running away."

"Felicitations, you accomplished that," Brodie snapped.

"Honestly Brodie, why are you always such an ass to me?"

Brodie stopped walking and turned around. "I'm an ass? I saved your bloody life tonight... twice, and what do I get? A stubborn wench who doesna ken when to listen. I had a plan, and you ruined it."

"Well, mayhap if you told me about your plan instead of hushing me up all the time, I would ken not to interfere," Orla replied.

"Well, mayhap if you just trusted me when I told you to stay put, I wouldn't have to shut you up all the time."

"Well, may—"

"Och, would ye both shut up. Now I wish ye'd shot me with an arrow too. Twould be less painful than listening to yer lovers' spat."

"We are not lovers!" They both shouted at the man hanging over Brodie's shoulder.

"Weil ye coulda fooled me."

"Silence!" Brodie said before knocking him out again.

Chapter 3 – The Wolf

The MacGregor Keep

The door to the Great Hall burst open as Brodie and Orla entered, arguing with raised voices.

"You will stay in the Keep tonight, Orla. I'll not have you in the woods alone."

"Brodie, I've already told you I'll be staying in my cottage after we deal with our prisoner."

"Either you stay in the Keep or I will move into your cottage with you. The choice is yours."

"Why are you two yelling in my hall like a pair of screeching banshees?" Chieftain Beiste MacGregor was scowling at the pair, standing with his arms folded.

Amelia, Beiste's wife, appeared behind him in a nightgown and shawl. "Keep your voices down. I just put the bairns to sleep and if either of you wakes them, I'll run you through."

"Who is that man over your shoulder?" Beiste asked.

"He just tried to kill Orla," Brodie replied.

Beiste tensed, then turned to his guardsman. "Fetch Dalziel, Kieran, and Rory. Tell them to meet us downstairs."

Amelia flew to Orla's side and started fussing over her. "Are you well? Did he hurt you? Do you have any wounds I need to tend? How dare he try to kill you?" She stomped her foot.

Amelia walked over to the unconscious man and slapped him hard across the face. She then grabbed Orla's arm and marched her towards the stairwell, ignoring her protests.

Before they disappeared out of view, Amelia paused and addressed the men. "I'll have a bath sent to your room Brodie because you reek of stinky perfume... and Beiste, try not to get blood on your shirt when you torture the prisoner. Tis impossible to clean."

Beiste rolled his eyes and muttered, "Daft woman."

Brodie just chuckled. He knew there was no way Amelia would let Orla leave the Keep tonight.

Dungeon

IT WAS WELL PAST MIDNIGHT when a select few were apprised of the threat. Men had gone to secure the woods and retrieve the body of the deceased. They had returned with two more bodies. Those of the missing MacGregor sentinels. Both had arrows through their chests.

Meanwhile, the assailant lay beaten and bloodied in the dungeon below the Keep.

Beiste and Brodie had been interrogating him for an hour, and he would not speak. His fear of retribution from the one who sent him was greater than the fear of the men before him.

They waited on Dalziel Robertson, Beiste's Second in Command. If anyone could torture information out of a man, it was Dalziel.

"Who sent you?" Brodie asked again.

"No one." The prisoner spat out blood when Beiste punched him.

"Why do they want Orla?" Brodie demanded.

"Perhaps they want to rut her like a whor—"

Brodie roared and knocked him out again before he could finish his sentence.

Moments later, the door to the dungeon swung open and Dalziel sauntered in. He wore trews and nothing else. His chest was bare. His long blonde hair parted and braided on both sides with leather ties. Dalziel held a dagger in each hand.

"Brothers, as heart-warming as it is to watch you both interrogate this swine, I think tis, time to administer something more interesting," he said with a part Angles part Scots accent.

"All yours," Beiste said and left the room.

"Just try not to kill him before you extract what you need," Brodie yelled as he ascended the stairwell.

Beiste and Brodie made it to the top of the dungeon stairs when they heard the piercing screams from the prisoner below.

Interrogation

DALZIEL THREW A BUCKET of water over the unconscious man, who shuddered. When he opened his eyes and saw Dalziel, he shook uncontrollably.

"Dear lord no. Not *the Wolf*! I swear... I swear I didn't tell them anything."

Dalziel's body tensed before he asked in a menacing voice. "Why did you call me the Wolf? Who sent you?"

The prisoner clasped his hands together as if in prayer. "Please... they said all I had to do was bring Vidar here and he would kill the lass. If I kenned, she had anything to do with the Wolf. I wouldn't have gotten involved, I swear it."

Dalziel calmly sat on a bench across from the prisoner. "Tis time we stopped playing games. Why did you call me the Wolf?" He started sharpening his daggers. The sound of blades scraping against each other was deafening in the quiet dungeon.

The prisoner sobbed. "I swear I dinnae ken anything."

Dalziel took a deep breath. "How about I make a deal? I'll set you free if you tell me who sent you and why they want the lass dead."

The man stopped mumbling and raised a speculative eye. "Ye'll let me go?"

"Aye. I will."

"No, you lie. The Wolf doesna have mercy."

Dalziel clenched his jaw at the reference. "This time, I'll make an exception. One name and a reason and you go free," he said.

The prisoner sniffed. "Really? Tis all I have to do."

"Aye. But on one condition."

"What's that?"

"You're going to tell me which finger you want me to cut off first." Dalziel grabbed the man's hand and placed it on the bench. Holding a sharp blade above the index finger, he asked, "This one?" Then he slammed the blade into the joint.

The prisoner began screaming.

Council Room

BRODIE AND BEISTE SAT in the Council Room, awaiting Dalziel and going through scenarios.

"Something is just not right. I can feel it. Tis like we are missing something crucial," Brodie said.

Beiste felt the same way when he replied, "Mayhap tis a jilted lover or someone of that nature? She was away for two months last summer."

Brodie stiffened and clenched his jaw. He would not think about Orla with any man.

An hour later, Dalziel sauntered into the room. He was wearing a clean shirt. He plonked himself in the chair beside Brodie and said, "The prisoner's name is Samuel. He is from Northumbria. An earl of

Orkney sent Vidar, the dead man, to find Orla. They were not to return until the deed was done."

Brodie sat stunned.

It raised even more questions for the men. For the first time, they realized how little they knew of Orla's background. All these years everyone had just accepted, she was an orphan.

"Where's the prisoner now?" Beiste asked.

"He's dead," Dalziel replied with a deadpan voice.

"Did you get carried away?" Brodie asked.

"He sealed his fate the moment he called me... the *Wolf*."

The room went silent.

"Bloody hell! What are we dealing with?" Brodie cursed.

Beiste said, "Bury the bodies. They were never here."

They all agreed.

"We need to question Morag. Tis important we ken everything about Orla and the night she arrived here," Dalziel said.

"When will Morag return from the Buchanan's?" Beiste asked.

One guardsman walked in. "Pardon me, Chieftain, but Morag is here in the Keep."

The Solar

ORLA WAS IN AMELIA'S solar with Jonet, Beiste's mother, and Sorcha, Beiste's sister. The four women had grown especially close over the past two years and worked together well, assisting Amelia in running the Keep.

"We should go see the prisoner. I want to ask him questions," Orla said as she paced the length of the hearth.

"No, Beiste made it clear we were not to interfere. They ken what they're doing, Orla," Amelia replied.

"Are you sure you are alright?" Sorcha asked.

"Aye, I was just shaken. Twas a good thing Brodie was there." Orla stopped pacing and stared at Sorcha.

"Sorcha MacGregor, is that rouge I see on your cheeks?"

Sorcha blushed. "Aye, Dalziel brought it from England on his last trip. He got some for me and Amelia."

Years ago, Sorcha had witnessed the murder of her father and lost her ability to speak until recently. She used to be very shy but was slowly becoming more open.

"Dalziel says the women there wear strange clothes and color their faces. He said they are not as bonny as Scottish lasses," Sorcha said.

"I think Dalziel is right. You dinnae need rouge to enhance your natural beauty," Amelia replied with a smile.

Orla could not help but notice how Sorcha was turning into a real beauty. Beiste had his work cut out for him, keeping suitors away.

"Ladies, enough talk of frivolous things. We have a mystery to solve," Jonet interrupted them.

Amelia nodded in agreement. "Aye, tis a mystery how Brodie was there with you… in the woods… in the dark… *alone*?"

Orla rolled her eyes. "I stumbled upon him coming out of Zelda's cottage."

Amelia looked as if she had swallowed a lemon. "I see. Then he is still a scandalous rogue," she said.

"Aye. But he was there in time or I would be dead."

"Do you ken who would mean to do you harm?" Jonet asked.

"No. Tis strange to me. I have no enemies I ken, at least none who would wish me dead."

"Mayhap tis someone from your past? Your kin maybe? It could be why your kin sent you here." Sorcha interjected.

"Aye, I have often wondered why they left me with the MacGregor clan."

"We need to speak with Morag about this. When does she return from *Stirlingshire*?" Amelia asked.

There was a knock at the door and Morag, Orla's adoptive mother, entered. Her grey cloak flying behind her, her wizened figure stooped over a crooked walking stick.

"Morag!" they all greeted.

"Ma, when did you get back?" Orla asked.

"I just arrived *mo nighean*. I left the Buchannan's as soon as I sensed you were in danger. Tis sorry I am that I was not here sooner."

"But the Buchannans are a day's ride. The attack only just happened," Sorcha said.

"Och, my visions have terrible timing. What tis the point of having the sight if I still arrive after the event?" Morag could always sense things before anyone else and often talked in riddles.

Jonet was already warming some tea for Morag and gave her a seat by the fire.

"Morag, do you ken who would want Orla dead?" Amelia asked.

Morag warmed herself by the fire and made a big production of stretching her limbs and cracking her bones. Then she launched into a long-winded rant.

"Och, the ride here twas long, and these old bones grow stiff and weary of that rickety cart. Tis 1042, for goodness sakes, and they still make cart benches out of hardwood. Can no one create something more comfortable for old women? Tis no wonder I am so sore. And it doesna help that my kin live so far away. Why cannot people just stay togeth—"

"Ma! Stop blathering and answer the question, please," Orla said, exasperated.

Morag sighed, "Och ye young'uns, always so impatient. I dinnae wanna start until the others get here because I'm sore out of breath."

"What others?" Jonet asked.

There was a great commotion at the door before it opened wide and Beiste, Dalziel, and Brodie walked into the solar.

Alone, they were a lot to take in, but together they were something else to behold. Their presence in the solar took up the entire space with such enigmatic force, Orla felt breathless.

Beiste strolled straight over to Amelia, scooped her up off her chair, while she shrieked in surprise, then sat down and settled her on his lap.

Brodie stood close to Orla and Dalziel took a seat near Morag, as he had many questions.

"I see this is to become a council meeting," Amelia said.

"Aye, love. We would like to ask Morag about Orla's past."

"See, I told ye we had to wait." Morag gave Orla a smug look.

"What about the prisoner? What did he have to say?" Amelia asked.

The men shook their heads slightly. It was an unspoken communication they would not discuss it in front of the others.

"What happened the night Orla was left on your doorstep, Morag?" Brodie asked first.

Morag replied, "It was as I've always said. Golden-haired men arrived. I assumed, by their dialect, they were Norsemen. They asked me to care for her and said they would return when the time was right."

"But why did they choose you?" Jonet asked.

"Their leader, the one who carried Orla on his shoulders. He said his wife read the runes and they pointed to me."

"You took Orla based on the words of a woman you've never met because she read the... runes?" Brodie asked incredulously.

"Aye."

"But why?" Beiste asked.

"Och weil now, ye see the week before Orla arrived. I had seen a vision of a wee lass standing at my door amidst a raging tempest. The wind was howling, the cottage was shaking, and the tempest was coming for her. I got the notion I was to shelter her until she was strong enough to face it."

"What does that even mean?" Brodie scoffed. "Someone is trying to murder Orla and we are sitting around listening to useless female witchery."

The women all glared at Brodie.

Beiste sighed. "Now you've done it."

Morag stood to her full height of... five foot zero... and pointed her staff directly at Brodie. "Dinnae scoff at me, Bear. Heed my words, the tempest has arrived and is coming for you as weil!"

"Och, I'm terrified, Morag," Brodie replied in a sarcastic tone.

"Shut up, Brodie!" everyone said in unison, except Orla, who kicked him in the shin instead.

Dalziel took a different approach and asked, "Morag, did Orla mention anything about her childhood when she first came here? Bairns often talk of places and people closest to them. Did she mention any names?"

"Aye, come to think on it, when she was a wee bairn, she often talked of a young man called 'Tor'. He gave her a puppy... and his ma's name was 'Runa'. I remember because it reminded me of the word rune." Morag paused, then stared at Dalziel with wonderment in her eyes, as if he just unlocked the secrets of the universe. "Och, weil look at ye Dalziel Robertson, ye sly fox. How ye got all that out of me so easily, tis impressive."

Morag turned to Brodie and snorted, "Unlike ye!"

Sorcha giggled.

"Orla, do any of these names mean anything to you?" Dalziel asked.

"I think I remember Tor... he was the most beautiful golden-haired boy I ever saw." Orla was smiling as if recollecting something.

Brodie growled and clenched his fists. "Who is this boy? Where do I find him?"

"Settle down," Beiste snapped.

Orla paced across the room as the memories came flooding back. "Runa was his ma and his da was... Hagan! That's it." She clicked her fingers. "I lived with them in a house by the sea with tunnels underneath and there was a longboat... we had to hide all the time. I never kenned why."

"Was it the Orkneys?" Brodie asked.

"No twas another place... close by... *Shetland*! It was called Shetland."

"Then that's where I'll start," Dalziel replied.

Everyone turned to look at him.

"I have business in the North. I can make some inquiries."

"What kind of business?" Sorcha asked.

"The kind you dinnae ask, and I dinnae tell, minx." He winked at Sorcha.

Orla suspected there was more behind his statement. Dalziel was a treasure trove of secrets.

The Way of Women

EVENTUALLY, MORAG, Jonet, and Sorcha sought their beds while the rest remained in the Solar discussing plans. Kieran and Rory joined them. They were two of Beiste's trusted guardsmen.

"I think tis best Orla remains in the Keep for the next few days just as a precaution. We dinnae ken if this earl will send more men," Brodie said.

Orla protested, "But I want to see what I can find in the woods. If there are more men, I can track them and—."

"You're no help to us dead," Brodie replied.

"I cannot stay locked up in here. Please let me come with you. I'll even let Kieran guard me." Orla grabbed Kieran's arm.

Kieran shook it off. "Och, no thanks. The last time I had to guard you, I ended up in the river with an itchy ass cause ye put poison ivy in me trews."

"How many times must I say it, Kieran? I didn't do it!" Orla huffed.

"Orla, someone tried to kill you and almost succeeded. This is not a negotiation. Tis decided," Brodie stated.

"What if Rory guards me while I'm in the woods?" Orla turned pleading eyes on Rory.

"Hmph... I'd rather guard Morag, she is less terrifying," Rory replied.

It was well known Rory was terrified of Morag because he continuously made the sign of the cross whenever she walked by.

Exasperated, Orla turned to Beiste. "Do you agree with Brodie?"

"I do, sorry Orla, but tis too dangerous for you to be out in the woods anymore."

Orla pleaded with Dalziel. "Dalziel? You ken I can be of use with my skills."

"Aye beauty, your skills are impeccable, but we cannot have men distracted trying to protect you and safeguard the woods."

Trust Dalziel to make sense, Orla thought.

"Amelia, what say you?" Orla turned to her best friend with hope in her eyes.

"I think, Sister, the men are right. Tis too dangerous. I prefer you remain closer to the Keep with me and the bairns."

Orla just glared at Amelia and placed both her hands on her hips. "Really?"

"Aye, tis for the best. Now, stop arguing, tis irritating!" Amelia glowered.

"Fine!" Orla looked around the room, shook her head, then walked out.

Amelia sighed. "I'll see to her. Dinnae worry she will come around to the decision that's in her best interest." Amelia smiled sweetly at the men, kissed Beiste on the lips, then left the room.

"Well, that was easy," Brodie said.

Beiste looked confused. "How so?"

"Amelia backed our decision, so Orla will listen for once."

Dalziel, Beiste, Kieran, and Rory all burst out laughing.

"What's so funny?" Brodie asked.

"Brother, for someone who has spent years bedding women, you dinnae ken a thing about them." Dalziel smirked.

"What do you mean?"

"Brodie, my wife, did not back our decision at all."

"But she just said she did." Brodie frowned.

"No, she just told us what *we* wanted to hear. I do not doubt as we speak, she and Orla are putting their heads together to find a creative way around it."

"Then you need to control your woman for her safety."

"Have you met my wife, Brodie?" Beiste snorted.

Brodie was rising from his chair.

"Where do you think you're going?" Kieran asked.

"To talk sense into both of them."

"You really are dense, Fletcher," Rory said.

"Well, aren't you going to stop them, Beiste?"

"Brodie, Brother..."—Beiste swung his arm over Brodie's shoulder—"let me give you a quick lesson on women like Amelia and Orla. The trick is to let them *think* we dinnae ken what they are planning. In the meantime, we take precautions to ensure whatever harebrained scheme they devise will not harm them."

"We'll increase their guards without their knowledge and recruit members of the staff to shadow them," Dalziel said.

"Aye," Kieran and Rory agreed.

Beiste said, "All you need to do, Brodie, is make sure you're close by in case Orla needs you."

"And this is your strategy for controlling women?" Brodie raised an eyebrow.

"No, tis my strategy for...love."

The Way of Men

MEANWHILE, A FLOOR below a similar conversation was in progress.

Amelia arranged a bath to be brought for Orla and ventured into the room.

"Why did you not back me, Amie? I cannot sit back and idly watch everyone else try to protect me!" Orla glared at her best friend.

Amelia strolled over to Orla and placed her arm across her shoulder. "Orla... Sister... let me give you a lesson on men like Beiste and Brodie. They need to *think* they are in control. So, we play along. In the meantime, we do as we please. Tis very simple what we *say* to the men is never what we *do*."

Orla grinned. "You ken whatever plan you come up with, Beiste will be one step ahead."

"Oh, ye of little faith. Tomorrow, we lie low, do not arouse any suspicion. Lull them into thinking we agree then when the time is right," — Amelia clapped her hands together— "we strike! Just leave everything to me."

Orla sighed and said, "That's what I'm afraid of."

Chapter 4 – Destiny

MacGregor Keep

Brodie could not sleep that night. He had bathed and eaten a light repast. He was staring out the window of his bedchamber when a knock came at the door.

"Enter."

Brodie recognized the serving woman. She was a buxom brunette, and she looked vaguely familiar. He was sure they must have trysted in the past.

"I have come to see if there was anything *else* you'll be needing tonight, Brodie?" she purred.

"No, thank you, Su... san?"

She did not react.

"Sar... ah?"

Still no reaction.

"Shar—"

"Tis Saundra."

"Aye Saun... dra," Brodie replied.

She gave him a seductive wink, then sashayed past him, ensuring her ample bosoms brushed up against his chest as she cleared the table.

Brodie knew what she was offering, but it only irritated him. He thanked her and dismissed her without a second thought. Saundra remained standing on the threshold, a surprised look on her face when Brodie quietly shut the door in her face.

Brodie was troubled. For the first time in his life, he was terrified at the prospect of loss.

When his mother abandoned him, he did not miss her because he knew she was safe wherever she was. When his father died, he felt no grief, only anger. When his grandparents passed, he did not mourn, for they were not close.

But when Brodie saw the arrow aimed at Orla, he felt an absolute fear of losing her. If she had died tonight, he would have mourned her forever. And that terrified him. Brodie made a vow to himself. He was done keeping his distance. Whether Orla liked it or not, he was her sworn protector. Starting immediately.

Night Terrors

THE NIGHT TERRORS DESCENDED with precision.

Orla had not had them for over a year but the attack in the woods must have triggered them again, taking Orla back to the fateful night a traitorous guardsman almost killed her. The vividness was there. Dark room, stone floor, cold, damp. She could still feel him groping her, biting her lips, kicking her ribs.

The smoke-like dream sequence faded, and Orla was somewhere else entirely. Somewhere her nightmares had never gone before. This time, Orla was in a large decadent room; she was in a bedchamber in an enormous castle. She saw herself as a babe. A woman was singing a melodic song to her in a strange language. The woman was mesmerizing, and her skin tone was like Orla's, only darker. She had familiar eyes. *Ma?*

She spoke to Orla saying, "Your *far* will be home tomorrow, little one, and he will be so happy to meet you."

But someone was standing in the shadows behind her. A man. He was not a good man. He held a knife and meant to hurt them. Her mother turned to face him. She pulled two swords out from under the mattress, holding one in each hand as she stood in front of Orla. A second man appeared, then a third. They were all armed, but their faces were blurry.

"Give me the bairn," the first man said with a scratchy throat.

"Never!" her mother replied and twirled the swords in a circular motion with her wrists, sizing up her opponents. She shifted her weight from one foot to the other. Staring at the three men. One lunged for her, but she was faster and sliced a deep gash across his chest. He yelled in pain and stepped back. The other two looked uncertain, then in unison, they moved to strike. The room filled with smoke. *Fire!* The dream faded.

"No!" Orla cried. "Dinnae hurt her, leave her alone!" Orla began thrashing and yelling, "Ma, come back!" She was struggling to run through the smoke, but her legs were heavy and lethargic. She started sobbing. Until she heard a deep voice she knew and cherished.

"Orla, wake up *mo leannan*. Wake up, tis just a dream." She felt arms holding her. A hand caressed her back as she calmed down. Orla opened her eyes and stared straight into a pair of umber-colored ones.

"Brodie?"

"Aye. Sweeting."

Orla realized she was awake in her bed and tucked into Brodie's side. His arm around her as they lay facing each other, her head resting against his shoulder.

"What are you—?"

Brodie placed a finger on her lips. "You were having a night terror. You are safe. I am here." He pushed an errant curl away from her face and kissed her forehead. "Go back to sleep, love."

Slightly dazed, she did not have the energy to resist and relaxed. Feeling safe and warm as the darkness receded. Her protector of old. The boy who stood between her and loneliness. He had returned. With those comforting thoughts, Orla drifted back to sleep.

When she woke again, Brodie was gone. A profound sense of disappointment assailed her that Brodie was just a dream, and yet the other side of her bed looked rumpled as if someone had lain there. She shook her head. It was impossible. *Brodie would never do that.*

Noting it was still early, Orla buried her head back in her pillow and slept.

Custard Tarts

SOMETIME LATER, ORLA awoke with the feeling of someone watching her.

When she opened her eyes, she saw a little face mere inches from her own, with one green and one brown eye.

"Iona MacGregor, why are you staring at me?" Orla asked.

"Aunty Orla, I need more arrows?"

"What happened to the ones I made last sennight *ban-dia*?"

"No, not those. I need sharp ones."

Orla had made Iona a set of bow and arrows. The ends had a soft cover so she could not do much damage, but Orla had also fashioned secret ones for her that had a sharpened edge.

Iona took to the bow like a seasoned warrior. Her concentration for a three, year-old was astounding. The bow was light, and she was becoming adept at her archery skills.

"Alright, I'll make you two more today," Orla replied.

"Are you sick?" Iona asked.

"No, I am not sick."

"Are you dying?"

"No, I am not dying."

"Are you sure?"

"Aye, I'm sure."

"Do you need some herb cream?"

"No, sweeting."

Iona was Beiste and Amelia's daughter. Given that her mother was also the clan healer, she had developed an unhealthy obsession with death and diseases.

"How long have you been standing there, Iona?"

"Since noonday's meal started. Grandma told me to come and get you because you didn't break your fast."

"What? It's noon?" Orla said in surprise.

"Aye and cook made custard tarts!" Iona beamed.

Orla shot up straight out of bed and gave Iona a quick kiss on her forehead. "Thank you for waking me, sweeting." She then scurried about getting ready while Iona ran through a list of diseases people can die from. When she was ready, she picked Iona up, and they hurried down the stairs.

"Aunty Orla, when Cook gives you your custard tart, can I eat it?"

"You can, sweeting."

"Yay!" Iona raised her arms in the air.

Orla suspected that was the only reason Iona agreed to wake her. The child was always sneaking food from her plate.

When they entered the hall, Kieran approached. "They have assigned me to guard ye all day today. Brodie's orders," he grumbled.

"Well, you can tell Brodie I dinnae care for his orders," Orla replied.

"Och, not this again. I am not getting in the way of another lovers' quarrel," Kieran said.

"Brodie and I are not lovers."

"That's what Beiste said about Amelia and look at what you're carrying in your arms right now," Kieran scoffed.

Orla responded, "Kieran, if you dinnae be quiet, I will put poison ivy in your trews again."

"Och, I kenned twas you!" Kieran rumbled as he trailed after her.

"Hello, glad you could join us." Jonet welcomed Orla to the high table on the dais.

Bethany, the cook, was serving up custard tarts. Orla sat down with Iona on her lap while Iona was eyeing the tarts, licking her lips.

"Where is everyone?" Orla asked Jonet as she picked at some fresh fruit on a platter.

"The men went out early this morn to notify the widows of the murdered sentinels. Amelia and Sorcha have gone with the women to gather provisions for the families. They'll be out most of the day," Jonet replied.

"Oh," Orla said, feeling sad for the men who died because of her. "I feel responsible."

Jonet said, "Tis not your fault, Orla. No one blames you. I'll be going there later. You should come with me."

Orla perked up, "Aye, that sounds—"

"Orla cannot leave the Keep," Kieran interrupted, taking a seat next to Orla.

"Surely just this once, Kieran, tis important," Jonet argued.

"No. She will remain in the Keep. I have my orders."

"Kieran?" Iona piped in. "Can I have your custard tart?"

"Aye lass." Kieran handed her his share and chuckled as he watched Iona stuff her face.

While Kieran was distracted, Jonet turned to Orla. "Amelia left some embroidering for you to do. Tis in her old bedchamber where she keeps her oak box." Jonet winked at her twice.

Orla hated embroidery but picked up the cue. "Aye, Amelia kens, how much I love to embroider in my spare time. I'll collect it after the meal."

Jonet nodded. "Mind ye check the oak box while you're there?" She winked again.

For the next hour, Kieran stuck to Orla like coos dung to a shoe. She could not retrieve the box. Orla became even more suspicious when Iona insisted, she play a game with her every ten minutes.

After the fifth game of hopscotch. Orla folded her arms and asked, "Iona, what did your Da promise you if you followed me around all day?"

"He didna promise me anything."

"Are you sure?"

"Aye... but Uncle Brodie did."

"And what was that?"

"He promised me four,"—she held up four fingers — "custard tarts and a toffee apple."

Blasted Brodie!

When Iona was having her afternoon nap, Orla gave Kieran the slip when he went to the privy. She found Amelia's box of treasures. Inside was a note with a small vile of valerian a plant used to make sleeping draughts. Amelia's note mentioned that Brodie, Beiste, and Dalziel would be away in the afternoon, which meant the coast was clear. There were guards in the woods, so Orla would be safe if she wanted to do some tracking, but she had to be quick.

When Kieran returned moments later, Orla asked if they could sit in the Great Hall and drink some cider. She would prepare a nice cold one for him. He agreed.

An hour later, Kieran was snoring in an armchair by the fire and Orla was nowhere to be seen.

Into the Woods

ORLA WAS ON HORSEBACK in the woods. She dismounted and was standing by the tree she had marked with her knife the previous night. It had been niggling her for some time. She crouched down and looked at the shoe prints again. It was as she thought. A large man had been in the woods sometime yesterday. The tracks were deeper on the right side, showing a limp as the weight came down harder on one foot.

She could recall no one with those characteristics within the MacGregor clan, which meant someone was in the woods who should not be.

Given the number of men securing the forest last night after her attack, it was almost impossible to pick up the tracks again, but she did, thanks to the larger footprints indented in the soil. The tracks lead deeper into the forest and towards the river.

It occurred to her, whoever it was, they were camping on the other side of MacGregor land, beyond the view of the sentinels. *But why?*

Orla stood wondering if she should venture out further or return to the Keep. Her instincts told her to keep going. But caution told her to wait. Regroup, notify the others, and live to track another day. Daylight was fading, and Amelia would get worried if she did not return. The last thing Orla wanted was a hunting party sent after her.

Orla decided she would head to her old cottage in the woods, have a quick wash in the Loch, then gather some of her belongings to take back to the Keep. She needed the familiarity of home, even for a short while.

By the time Orla was safely inside her cottage and freshly bathed, the sun was just setting. Orla realized she was famished. She got a fire started and made some tea with cheese and bread. She was enjoying her repast when Morag entered.

"Ma, what are you doing here?"

"Och, I could ask ye the same question. I was heading home and saw yer fire."

"Are you not staying in the Keep tonight?" Orla asked.

"I dinnae like Keep life, tis too noisy and the bed tis too hard on these old bones. I didna sleep weil."

"Then join me for tea and warm yourself by the fire."

"Dinnae mind if I do."

The two women fell into a comfortable rapport. But amid their conversation, Morag's eyes glazed over before she gripped Orla's forearm and sat up straight.

"The golden hair... they have returned. Ye must go with them. There is danger if ye stay."

"Ma." Orla tried to pry her arm free of Morag. "What do you mean?"

"Tis time to find out who ye are, tis your destiny." Having spoken those words, Morag relaxed and continued sipping her tea and chatting as if nothing had happened.

Orla just sat quietly and tried to process the information. She was used to Morag's premonitions, but it still unsettled her.

Eventually, Morag stood and gathered her cloak. "Och weil, I best be on me way. I dinnae wanna be around for this part."

Orla asked, "What part?"

Morag did not answer her. She left hastily and was out the door so fast, before Orla could stop her.

It was then Orla heard the thunderous roar of horses' hooves. Moments later, the cottage door was flung wide open, and Brodie stood in the doorway looking beyond livid.

"Damn it to hell, Orla! What are you doing here?" he yelled.

Orla could see several MacGregor retainers outside. They all had scowls on their faces, including Kieran, who was glaring at her.

Feeling like a child who had been caught sneaking sweets from the pantry, Orla stammered, "I... uh..."

Before any other words could come out. Brodie slammed the door shut behind him and stalked towards her. Orla shuffled backward until she could feel the table press against her bottom.

Brodie stopped directly in front of her. "You drugged Kieran, then you went into the woods to the edge of MacGregor land. Did it ever occur to you that you were placing your life in danger?" He seethed.

Orla opened her mouth to say something.

"Shut it!"

She shut her mouth as Brodie continued.

"Not only did you go against my attempts to protect you, you then, come here and drink tea like a princess with no concern that I have been searching for you... for half a day!" He roared the last four words.

"But I thought you were away?" Orla bit her tongue, knowing she had just implicated Amelia.

Brodie clenched his jaw and folded his arms across his chest. "No, that's what we told Amelia."

Orla talked fast. "Brodie, it wasn't her fault. I needed to look at the tracks I found yesterday. There's something there. I had every intention of coming back before nightfall—"

"Yet here you are and tis nightfall," he said sarcastically, lifting his arm and gesturing towards the window that framed the view of the night sky.

His tone grated on Orla's nerves. Rather than try to placate him, which had been her intention, she felt her anger rising in return. "I'm sorry if I caused you trouble, but there is no need to speak to me like I'm a wee bairn."

They stood glaring at each other in silence. Finally, Brodie turned and stormed out of the cottage. Orla heard him issuing orders outside to the retainers. The men dispersed and Brodie left.

Orla breathed a sigh of relief. Her run-in with Brodie was having an unwelcome effect on her. It was making her hot and bothered. The more they sparred, the more attracted she was to him to the point all she could think about was grabbing his stupid face, climbing him like a tree, and kissing him senseless. She needed to get control of her riotous emotions.

Her relief was temporary, however, when Brodie entered the cottage sometime later, slamming the door shut and locking it. His hair was wet, he had bathed in the loch. Brodie held a travel sack in his hand, which he dropped on the floor without taking his eyes off her.

The look on Brodie's face was heated and feral. He was breathing heavily and staring at her in a way that made her nipples harden and her quim feel as if it would burst into flames.

He then pulled off his shirt and stood before her bare-chested. And glory be. Orla thought it was the most awe-inspiring muscular chest she had ever seen. *Bards should write ballads about that torso.* He had battle scars in some places, but they only added to the rugged appeal.

"Brodie... er... what are you doing?" she stammered.

"What does it look like, minx? If you willna stay in the Keep, then I will stay in here with you."

"You cannot stay here?" She winced at the high-pitched panic in her voice.

"I am keeping my eyes on you at all times from now on," he replied.

"But there's only one bed."

"So?"

"Where will you sleep?"

"In it, with you."

"I dinnae think tis necessary, I can just return to the Keep." Orla sprinted for the door, but Brodie prevented her escape by lifting her and throwing her onto the bed.

"Take off your clothes, love, tis time for bed," he whispered.

"Such romantic words, Brodie, how the women must gasp and swoon," Orla bit out.

Brodie was barely keeping it together. Orla was killing him. He was so hard. Brodie was gritting his teeth. He had spent half the day worried sick over her whereabouts and to find her casually drinking tea in her cottage brought out the bear in him. The constant need to claim her as his warred with his intention to keep a safe distance. He had intended to drag her to the Keep, but in the past half-hour, he had changed his mind. The only way to protect her was to do it himself. He cursed Kieran for falling for the oldest trick in the book.

Brodie shook his head. No, he could not trust her safety with anyone else anymore. She was too precious to him.

"I'll not ravish you, Orla, but I need to rest and there is no way I am letting you sleep fully clothed so you can escape in the night."

Orla was trying to keep the panic out of her voice. But she *was* panicking. There was no way she was sleeping naked next to Brodie. That way led to ruin. It was too intimate, too dangerous. She had opened her heart before and had it trampled on. She was not about to let her traitorous body lead her astray.

"Truce!" she yelled. "I'll share the bed on two conditions."

"I'm listening."

"I wear a leine and we keep pillows between us at all times so there is no touching."

"Agreed. Now come to bed," Brodie said immediately, although he had no intention of honoring the deal.

It turned out Orla was the one who broke the agreement because when Brodie woke in the middle of the night; he found her half sprawled on top of him, fast asleep. He chuckled, tucked her into his side like he did the night before in the Keep... and went back to sleep.

Chapter 5 – The Missive

The next morning, it relieved Orla to find Brodie gone when she awoke. She quickly got out of bed, warmed some water, washed, and dressed. She opened the door to see if anyone was outside and was greeted by Lachlan, a guardsman.

"Good morn Orla," he said.

Orla smiled. "Morning Lachlan. Have you seen Brodie?"

"Aye, he is at the Keep. Ye'll need to stay indoors until he returns."

"Can I at least step outside and get some fresh air?"

"No, but ye can open a window and stick your head out of it." Lachlan quipped.

Orla just rolled her eyes. "Dinnae get smart with me, Lachlan. Where is Kieran?"

"Kieran is on garderobe cleaning duty for the next three days."

"I spose he willna be happy with me for some time."

"Aye, and I dinnae wish to join him. So, unless you knock me unconscious, you willna be getting past this door." He stood, legs apart and arms folded, blocking her way.

Orla just huffed and returned inside.

She was going to go insane, cooped up in the cottage. She needed to follow those tracks. Orla opened the tiny back window and stared out into the woods. Then a thought occurred to her. Maybe she could fit through it if she twisted her body at the right angle.

She had just placed both hands on either side of the frame when a stern voice startled her. "Dinnae even think about it!"

Orla peeked out the window and saw Rory leaning against a tree.

Blasted Brodie, the man thought of everything!

Back at the Keep

BRODIE HAD RECEIVED an urgent message that morning that they needed him at the Keep. When he walked into the Great Hall, he saw Amelia storming towards him.

"There you are, you cur!" Amelia punched him in the arm, winced in pain, then kicked him in the shin.

"What have I done now?"

"You are a rogue and a scoundrel. How dare you?" She fumed.

"How dare I do what?"

"Seduce Orla and ruin her reputation." Amelia hissed before kicking him again.

"Amelia, stand down, love, before you break a limb," Beiste said as he strolled towards them. "Twould seem my wife heard rumors you slept in Orla's cottage last night, Brodie."

"What of it? I dinnae deny it."

"Brother, surely you can find other women to dally with."

Brodie was getting angry. It was one thing to insult him; it was quite another to compare Orla with women from his past. "Nothing happened. I guarded her during the night to ensure her safety and I will spend every night in her cottage, if that's what it takes to protect her."

"I ken the likelihood of you and Orla trysting is minimal, but your reputation alone places her at risk of gossip and censure," Beiste said.

"Aye, twas the talk of the serving women this morning that you are now warming her bed." Amelia frowned, placing both hands on her hips.

Brodie looked surprised. He had not contemplated how staying overnight in Orla's cottage would look to the others. The last thing he wanted was to ruin her reputation.

"Fine, I will do right by her."

"And what do you mean by that?" Amelia asked.

"Fetch Abbot Hendry. There's going to be a wedding," Brodie replied.

"Wait a minute, Brodie, dinnae be hasty now," Amelia said with a concerned expression.

"Mistress, you just told me Orla's reputation is ruined, so I mean to fix it."

"Aye, but I didn't think you would marry her. I just wanted you to stay away. Orla deserves someone…"

"Someone what?" Brodie folded his arms and waited for an explanation.

"She deserves someone who will be *faithful* to her and not bed other women."

"And what is your point?" Brodie asked, clenching his jaw.

Amelia hesitated then said, "Well… tis just that uh… Beiste, willna allow it!"

"I won't?" Beiste looked confused.

Amelia glared at her husband and elbowed him in the rib.

"Aye, just like Amie says, I cannot allow it," Beiste said.

"Why not?" Brodie asked while staring daggers at Beiste.

Beiste looked between Amelia and Brodie, both giving him the evil eye. "Bloody hell, I dinnae ken why!" He looked exasperated. "This conversation is confusing me. Twas, not even the reason I called you to the Keep."

Amelia rolled her eyes and gave Brodie a stern look. She pointed her finger at him. "You willna marry Orla. I forbid it. Now if you'll excuse me, I have crofters to visit and I will take the fifty guardsmen Beiste has trailing me around all day."

"Tis not fifty guardsmen, dinnae exaggerate, wife," Beiste scoffed.

"Fine, forty-nine then." Amelia stood on tiptoe, kissed Beiste on the cheek, and marched out of the hall.

Brodie just shook his head, not understanding what had just happened. "So, what was the real reason you called me here, Beiste?"

"Come with me. Dalziel is in the study. We can discuss it there."

When they entered, Brodie saw Dalziel going over letters.

"Glad you could join us," Dalziel greeted.

"What is this about?"

They took their seats, and Beiste explained. "A missive arrived this morning from Amelia's *seanáthair*, Gilleain Maclean. Norsemen have been raiding and pillaging the Hebrides. The Macleans have their hands full protecting the Isles."

Dalziel continued where Beiste left off. "Gilleain warns one of his spies reported the raiders were looking for a woman. Tis rumored she is the *nighean* of a powerful jarl. Her existence has caused a great deal of strife between the earls of Orkney."

"Did the raiders mention who she was?"

"Only that she was... mixed race, and there was something about a fire years ago and a missing bairn," Beiste replied.

Brodie stiffened and started clenching his fists. "What else did he say?"

Beiste continued, "Gilleain remembered meeting Orla here last summer, and the fact she was an orphan and rumored to have Viking blood caused him concern. He warns raiders are on the move with orders to kill her."

"I will increase the sentinels and guards. Warn the crofters. Gather people into the Keep and reinforce the walls," Brodie said.

Dalziel responded, "Aye, tis a sound plan. I am waiting for word from the North. I have men there who can get me information faster. Dinnae worry, Brother, we will keep Orla safe."

Before they went their separate ways, Brodie stopped them. "Wait, there is something else that needs to be done."

"What is it?" Beiste asked.

"I have thought about what Amelia said out in the hall. She is right. I cannot protect Orla without ruining her reputation. Which is why I mean to marry her."

"Since when does anyone listen to Amelia?" Dalziel looked at Brodie like he had lost his mind.

Beiste agreed. "Aye, she's my wife, and I dinnae even listen to her half the time."

"Orla is in danger. I want her to have the protection of my name and I want the right to fight anyone who comes between us," Brodie replied.

Brodie thought about Orla as his wife, and he experienced none of the panic he usually did when he thought about marriage and being tied to one woman for eternity. In fact, he felt the opposite. He could not imagine a life without her in it. *Was that love?*

"Then I'll arrange it. But Amelia willna be pleased," Beiste said with a sigh.

"Tis, not Amelia I intend to please," Brodie replied. "There is one more thing. I need both your backing on this."

"Name it," Dalziel said.

"I want Kieran to have Orla's room."

Cottage Life

AMELIA MADE A SURPRISE visit to Orla to see how she was faring.

"Orla, I needed to make sure you are all right?"

"Aye, I am well. Although I am being held prisoner in my cottage by an idiot." Orla shouted the word 'idiot' so Lachlan could hear. He just snorted.

"Orla, I am sorry Beiste tricked me. I assumed they were away for the afternoon, but they were only just in the village. Of all the underhanded things to do. That man kens me too well."

"I told you, Amie, he is always a step ahead of you. But now you are here, I have news. I found tracks yesterday leading to the edge of MacGregor land. I tried to tell Brodie about it, but we just ended up... never you mind."

"Ended up what, Orla? Spit it out."

"Nothing, he just insisted we sleep in the same bed and I forgot to pursue the matter."

Amelia raised an eyebrow. "And did you just sleep in the same bed? or *sleeeep* in the same bed."

"We slept as in with eyes closed and no naked parts touching."

"Good, because, Orla, we all ken Brodie's reputation with the ladies, and I dinnae want you to be another notch on his bedpost."

"Tis no fear of that Amie, I despise the man." Orla lied. "But I dinnae want to talk about Brodie."

"Aye, sorry, tell me about the tracks."

"Amelia, I think people are camping on the other side of the borderline. I believe one of them to be a large man with a limp. If I can kidnap him, I will have more answers about who is trying to kill me."

"Kidnap him? Orla, are you daft? You cannot capture a giant." Amelia looked horrified.

"Aye, I will, and you are going to help me."

"Orla... I dinnae like the sound of this."

Beyond the Borderline

THE SWITCH WAS EASY enough to achieve. Amelia had sent one of her guards to fetch Morag for tea. Ten minutes later, Orla left the cottage wearing Morag's hooded cloak while Amelia and Morag remained in the cottage.

Lachlan was none the wiser, and Rory was terrified of Morag, so he did not question her.

Orla was now standing in the same spot she was the day before. She stared across the borderline between MacGregor land and the woods leading to the river. Before she could second guess herself, she left her horse grazing and crossed the borderline on foot.

It was easy enough to pick up the tracks again, so Orla followed. If anyone watched, they would assume she was an old crone wandering the hillside.

By midday, Orla had come across an old campsite, the embers of the fire losing their glow. It was there she found more footprints of various sizes accompanying the larger tracks. There were four of them altogether. She studied the direction of their movements. The tracks were still fresh, which meant she needed to hurry.

She came to a river and kept walking through an area of dense vegetation. Pushing her way through heavy thickets, she tripped on a tree root and stumbled forward, straight into a clearing and a group of men setting up camp.

Time stood still as they stared at her and she at them. The men had golden hair. She noted an enormous giant amid them. He held a bundle of firewood. His mouth was ajar, with a look reflecting her own. Beside him was a breathtakingly handsome man who was stunning. A classically chiseled face framed his blue eyes, and his muscular arms bore strange inked markings. He was so attractive, Orla imagined he had fallen from heaven. All that was missing was angels' wings.

Orla slowly retreated, taking one step backward before she spun around and ran.

"Git her!" She heard one shout before they were hot on her heels, crashing through the forest. They were talking in a dialect that seemed familiar. *Norsemen.*

Orla was inwardly cursing her own stupidity now for venturing out on her own. *What was she thinking, trying to capture a seven-foot limping giant?*

She could hear them gaining on her. Her only chance was to dive into the river and swim. Orla had just made it to the riverbank when arms like steel banded around her from behind. She tried to stomp on her captor's foot, but he overpowered her. She had her weapons under the cloak and could not reach her dirk, so instead, she jerked her head backward in the hope of head-butting him in the face. Given the height difference, she only grazed his chin.

Her captor chuckled. "Whit, is dis? A feisty wench?" He twirled her around to face him as her hood fell, revealing her face. They both froze.

Orla came face to face with the handsome Angel and up close he was... breathtaking. He tilted his head to the side as if scrutinizing her; he straightened and then he broke out into a wide smile. It was at that moment Orla recognized him.

"Tor?"

"Aye, peedie bird. I've come to rescue ye."

Before she could register anything else, he had wrapped his arms around her and pulled her close. He then bent his head down and tilted her chin up before his lips connected with hers.

And that was when all hell broke loose.

Chapter 6 – Return of the Golden-Hair

Torstein Hagansson and his men had been lying low just outside of MacGregor land for two days. They were waiting for the right moment to extract Orla with as little disruption as possible. Tor was not in the habit of murdering innocent people, but if they got in his way, he would stop at nothing to complete his mission.

They were in place to kidnap Orla when the assassination attempt occurred, and with security being stepped up, they found it almost impossible to get to her again.

Torstein felt the need to claim her as his own and protect her. This would explain why, instead of grabbing her and galloping off to Dunsinane, he was instead kissing her as if his life depended on it. He just could not resist her succulent lips. If they were alone, and she was receptive, he would take her right here on the riverbank. Such was the need she aroused within him.

Torstein coaxed Orla's lips apart. When she opened her mouth, he pushed his tongue inside and licked her lips. He heard her moan, and then she was kissing him back. That sent a surge of heat to his groin and next, he knew he had her backed up against a tree, both hands in her hair, holding her in place so he could deepen their kiss.

He tried to drown out his men mumbling in the background, especially the giant Njal in his deep gravelly voice saying, "Whit is dis? I thought we werna allowed to ravage our captives?"

He heard Mathias say, "Tor is protecting her."

"Tis not possible to protect someone with yer lips," Aksel grumbled.

Orla responded to the kiss. She grabbed Tor's forearms to steady herself. Orla closed her eyes as he nipped at her lips. She sighed and whispered, "Mmm, Brodie..."

Torstein stilled. "Who's Brodie?"

Orla's eyes shot open. She gasped and pushed him away. He tried to pull her back into his arms when he heard swords being drawn and a voice bellow, "Get your hands off my wife!"

Torstein spun around and pushed Orla behind him. He drew his weapon.

Despicable Demigods

BRODIE SAW RED. HE had discovered Orla's escape plan just in time and rode out with several retainers. Lachlan and Rory were now scrubbing garderobes right alongside Kieran. Amelia was at the Keep getting a stern talking-to from Beiste and once Brodie got through with matters here, he was tying Orla to his bed indefinitely.

Although that is not why he was furious. It was the possessiveness he felt witnessing another man kissing *his* woman and his woman *returning* the kiss. Brodie gritted his teeth. He was jealous, and Brodie Fletcher never got jealous, until now.

He was going to have to step up his wooing efforts because there was no way he was letting some golden-haired, braw, ruggedly handsome, impeccably dressed, demigod sweep in and seduce his woman from under him. He knew this was penance for his past womanizing ways. But he was ready to fight to the death.

"Orla, come here now!" Brodie yelled, wielding his axe and sword.

"She's not gan anywhere with ye," Torstein shouted in return.

"I am talking to my wife. Stop interfering," Brodie shouted.

Torstein asked Orla over his shoulder, "Is it true? Are ye married to that big troll?"

"No, but he has been protecting me. Since I was a child."
"I take it his neem is Brodie?"
"Aye."
Torstein sighed. "Are ye gan' talk about our kiss?"
Orla said, "I'd rather not, thanks."
"Weil, was it a wonderful kiss?"
"Twas nice, but..."
"Yer heart wasn't in it?"
"Oh Tor, I cannot explain, but I feel connected to that loud brute over there."
"Is he a reasonable man?"
"Most of the time."
"But not when it comes to you?"
"He can be a little..."
"Possessive? I dinnae blame him."
Brodie growled, "Are you two going to chat amongst yourselves all day?"
"Calm down, Brodie, I'm coming out. Dinnae hurt these men. They mean no harm," Orla shouted.

Decisions

AN HOUR LATER, THEY gathered in the Council Room. The MacGregors and Torstein and his men agreed they needed to work together. First, they needed to know what they were up against.

Brodie still wanted to behead the disgustingly pretty man for kissing Orla, but for the sake of peace, he would let it be.

In the meantime, Brodie seated Orla beside him and placed Torstein at the far end of the table. Brodie also made a point of draping an arm over Orla's shoulder, even though she kept trying to shrug it off.

"Brother, why dinnae you just piss on her chair so no one will come close?" Beiste said with a chuckle as Dalziel stifled a laugh.

Brodie just glared at them. He wanted to punch them in the face. *Smug bastards.* He was overreacting, but he had never felt this level of possessiveness towards any woman before. He wanted the world to know Orla was his.

Eventually, the room quietened when Torstein stood to address the group. "An earl from Shetland, Rognvald Brusisson, has sent men to kill Orla. They willna stop coming until she is dead."

"But why?" Amelia asked.

Mathias, one of Torstein's men, answered, "Tis because of her *far*."

"Who is her da?" Beiste asked.

"He is... Thorfinn Sigurdsson, Jarl of Orkney."

Everyone tensed and turned to stare at Orla. There were looks of consternation and disbelief.

Orla followed the exchange, transfixed. She had never heard of Thorfinn but could tell the MacGregors had, and they were not happy.

Beiste looked stunned. "I dinnae believe it. Orla's da, is Thorfinn *'the Mighty'*?"

Torstein nodded.

Dalziel stood up abruptly and started pacing the room and rubbing his beard. An incredulous look replaced his usually calm demeanor. "Your people hid her here and didn't think to tell us?"

Torstein looked contrite. "Twas a decision my parents made. The less anyone kenned, the easier it was to keep her hidden... and it has worked so far."

"But why? What is the reason this earl wants her dead?" Brodie asked.

"Because he is partly responsible for her *mor's* death," Aksel said.

Orla gasped and tears started spilling from her eyes without her realizing it.

Brodie reached across and held her hand. Orla gripped it firmly, as if it were a life raft to a drowning sailor.

"What is it you want us to do?" Beiste asked.

"I need to get her to Macbeth," Torstein replied.

"How does this involve Macbeth?" Brodie asked.

"Thorfinn is his first cousin through their grandfather, Malcolm. They are close and Macbeth is the only one who can find the jarl."

"Why does he need to find him?" Dalziel asked.

Torstein took a deep breath, "Thorfinn doesn't ken he has a dattar. He believes his lover and his bairn perished in a fire. That is whit the earls told him. But with Orla alive, it raises questions."

"Wait, who was Orla's ma?" Amelia interrupted.

"A foreigner. Her name was Izara, she was Thorfinn's thrall," Njal replied.

Orla felt as if someone had pushed the air out of her lungs. She sat silently listening to the news, but also feeling detached from everyone in the room. For years, she had yearned for her own family, and now the revelations left more questions unanswered. It was too overwhelming.

Brodie lifted her hand to his lips and kissed the back of it. "All will be well, love," he whispered in her ear. Orla found great comfort in his gesture and smiled in return.

Torstein watched the interplay between Brodie and Orla and realized he had no chance of winning her because the lumbering ox beside her had already claimed her heart.

"So, Orla, is King Malcolm's great-granddaughter?" Amelia asked.

"Aye," Torstein answered.

Amelia looked at Orla. "Sister, this makes us true kin. King Malcolm was also my great grandfather."

Both women shared a tender moment at the revelation.

Brodie did not like the sound of this. If Orla was Macbeth's kin, Macbeth could deny their marriage.

"Those who seek to kill Orla do so to prevent Thorfinn from finding out she is alive. The way to eliminate the threat is to find him and introduce him to his *dattar*," Torstein said.

"Then I suggest we send Orla and a contingent of warriors to Dunsinane," Beiste replied, ending the meeting.

They agreed everyone remained in the Keep for safety. There would be no more trips to the woods. They also made plans to leave at first light.

They sent a missive to Dunsinane to inform Macbeth that the MacGregors would seek a special audience with him within the sennight.

On the way out of the room, Torstein used the opportunity to sidle up to Orla. "Do you need me to guard you tonight, peedie bird? I would happily warm your bed." He winked at her.

Orla chuckled and was about to respond when Brodie pulled her to his side and hissed at Torstein. "I suggest you find another bed to warm... you... despicable demigod!"

Brodie marched Orla out of the room and missed the smirk on Torstein's face. Torstein decided if he could not win Orla, then he would make himself as disagreeable to her big ogre as possible.

Rearrangements

ORLA WAS EXHAUSTED when she retired to her room. She just wanted a bath and some food and her nice warm bed. She threw open her door and stilled. Mouth agape in shock, she stared at the empty room.

"Where are my things?"

"In my room."

She turned and saw Brodie behind her.

"Why?"

"Because I need to protect you and you now sleep with me."

"Brodie Fletcher, you had no right taking my things."

"Why do you do that?"

"Do what?"

"You always call me by my full name when you're annoyed."

"Because your full name irritates me," Orla replied.

"That makes no sense, love. I am the least annoying person in the world."

Orla just rolled her eyes. "Well, you can just return all my things, Brodie Fletcher, because I willna be sleeping in any room other than my own." Orla huffed with her hands on her hips.

"Och sorry love, tis impossible now."

At that moment, people entered with furnishings and trunks. They shoved Orla out of the way.

"What is happening?" she asked.

"I'm moving in." Kieran appeared behind her with his arms full of clothes.

"No! Tis my room and I am still using it."

"Ye should have thought of that before you drugged me." Kieran dumped his clothes on the rug and went about rearranging furniture.

"We shall see about that, Kieran MacKenzie!" Orla stormed out of the room in search of Amelia.

Brodie followed behind her, chuckling. "See, I told you I'm not the most irritating person in the world."

"What are you talking about, Brodie?" Orla gritted her teeth.

"Well, you just called Kieran by his full name, which means he irritates you just as much."

Orla gave him a quelling look and kept walking. "Please go away. I dinnae need your shadow blocking my sunlight."

"Tis night-time." Brodie grinned when he heard her cursing under her breath.

He had to admit, the view of Orla storming away was a sight to behold. Watching her curvy bottom march down the hall did nothing to cool his ardor.

"Where precisely are you going?" he asked.

"To see Amelia. She needs to end this nonsense."

"Wait. I wouldn't do that, love."

"You cannot stop me, Brodie. I ken she will see reason."

"No, I mean tis, not a good time. I saw Beis—"

"Stop following me, Brodie," Orla snapped. "Amelia needs to put a stop to this nonsense."

"Dinnae say I didn't warn you," Brodie smirked.

Without knocking, Orla threw the door wide open and burst into Amelia's Solar. Then instantly regretted it when she saw Beiste and Amelia partially naked and engaging in a very amorous bout of lovemaking against the wall.

Holding the door handle, she stood in stunned silence. At first, she was shocked to walk in on such an intimate scene. Then she was curious that people could engage in such activity against a wall.

Amelia gasped at the sight of Orla.

Beiste growled, "Bloody hell! Does nobody knock in this blasted Keep?"

The couple rapidly tried to disengage from one another and right their clothing.

Orla blushed. "I'm sorry. I'll uh..." She backed out of the room and slammed the door shut. Covering her face, mortified, she stood in the hallway trying to unsee what she just saw.

She could hear Amelia giggling uncontrollably. Then Beiste grumbled, "Tis, not funny Amie, I could've dropped you and injured my man-parts." Then Orla heard Amelia burst out laughing and Beiste cursing.

Orla heard a chuckle coming from behind her. Brodie was leaning against the wall in the hallway with his arms folded, legs crossed, just looking at her. "I told you not to go in there."

"You could have been more specific."

"Orla, everyone in this Keep kens the chieftain cannot keep his hands off his wife. Not since the first day, he saw her in that dusty village." Brodie walked towards her. "Which is why everyone knocks before entering any room those two are in."

"Well, I didn't realize they'd be *at it* in the solar."

"They're married and they're deeply in love, Orla. They are bound to go at it whenever the need arises."

"But they're married with bairns."

Brodie was now standing directly in front of her. "They're married, not dead."

Soon, the door to the solar opened and Beiste stormed out, scowling at Orla before walking away.

Amelia came to the door, smiling with a slight blush. "You can come in now, Sister."

"Amelia, I am so sorry for interrupting you and Beiste."

"Dinnae feel bad Orla, Beiste and I will pick up where we left off later." Amelia winked at her and ushered her inside.

Brodie barged his way in, deciding it was time to put an end to Orla's reservations.

"What's the matter, Orla?" Amelia asked.

"You need to assign me a different room other than the one he's in." She pointed her thumb at Brodie.

"I cannot do that, Orla. The rooms have been allocated, and Beiste told me he needs his guardsmen in the Keep."

"Fine, I'll go stay in my cottage."

"You need to remain in the Keep," Amelia said.

"Then I'll... build my own Keep."

"Beiste cannot spare the stones," Brodie replied smugly.

Brusi's Island, Shetland

"IS SHE DEAD?" EARL Rognvald Brusisson asked his kinsman, Moddan.

"No."

"Then why are ye here?"

"She does not know who her *far* is or who her kin are. We should just leave well alone," Moddan said.

"As long as she's alive, she poses a risk."

"Tis a minimal risk, my lord."

"The jarl is raiding Alba and the Isles because of his appetite for destruction. Do ye ken whit turned him into that man?" Rognvald asked.

"No."

"Losing his lover and his bairn. Whit, do ye think he would do if he found out what we did?"

"Chances are minimal. Ye could bring his attention to her by pursuing this path."

Rognvald crossed the dais in an instant, stopping just in front of his kinsman. "Ye ken the jarl is a shrewd, violent man? It willna take him long to figure out whit happened and then ye and I will no longer be breathing."

"I understand but—"

"He'll not only kill us, Moddan; he'll torture us and no doubt lop off your other hand."

They both looked down at Moddan's handless arm.

Rognvald said, "We cannot assume the protection of Norway. So, make sure she is dead, or ah'll see the spiked heads of your family lining the shores of *Bressay*."

"I'll make sure of it." Moddan sighed.

"What of Runa and Hagan?" Rognvald asked.

"They have disappeared."

"And Torstein?"

"He left by longboat a few days ago."

"And your man was with him?"

Moddan replied, "Aye. He was with them and he'll do his part."

That answer satisfied Rognvald. Moddan would see the job done.

Chapter 7 – Fools Rush In

When everyone had retired to their beds for the night. Orla had bathed and was wearing a chemise with a woolen *airisaidh* draped around her shoulders. She was drying her hair by the fireplace when Brodie entered their chambers. His long hair was partially wet, and she could scent lye soap. He had bathed in the Loch.

"Brodie, we cannot keep sharing a bed," she said.

"As long as golden-haired men roam about the place, I intend to sleep in the same bed with you."

Orla sighed. "Brodie, people will gossip about us."

"Why?"

"Because we are not married, and they ken I am sharing your bedchamber."

"Well, I intend to change that."

"How?"

Brodie cleared his throat and said, "I think tis high time we married."

"What? Have you been drinking, Brodie?" Orla sniffed his neck.

"I have not had a single drop."

"Did you get too much sun?" Orla felt his forehead with the back of her hand.

"I am serious, Orla. I have already discussed it with Beiste, and he agrees, marriage tis the best way to protect you."

Orla just stared at him. "Are you daft? We cannot marry?"

"Why not?"

"Because we hate each other, Brodie."

"I dinnae hate you, Orla. I never have." Brodie stared at her with a soft expression that had Orla feeling somewhat uncomfortable.

"Marriage is a big step, Brodie, not to be taken lightly."

"Look at me." Brodie stepped in front of Orla. "We need to marry right now before we leave for Macbeth's castle." Brodie grabbed her hand and headed for the door.

"Where are we going?"

"The chapel is ready. Abbot Hendry is waiting."

"You cannot just decide this, Brodie, tis more at stake. You haven't even asked me."

Brodie turned around, got down on one knee, and asked, "Orla, will you marry me?"

"No!" she replied.

Brodie stood and placed his hands on her shoulders. "Orla, the best protection is for us to marry and for it to be legally binding. That way, I can be with you wherever you go in the castle because I am your husband."

Orla thought about what he said. It would make sense to have his protection. But what happened once the threat disappeared? What then?

"Brodie dinnae sacrifice your freedom to keep me safe."

"Tis no sacrifice."

"Will this be a marriage in name only?" Orla asked.

"Absolutely not," Brodie grimaced. "I intend to bed you as often as I can."

Orla just blushed.

"But what of children, Brodie? What happens if we go our separate ways after the risk is over?"

"I will acknowledge any bairn that results from our union no matter what happens."

Orla did not want to bring children into such a loveless marriage.

"No, if we do this, I will ask Amie to give me herbs that can prevent your seed from taking root. Not that I am even contemplating marrying you yet," Orla said.

Brodie stiffened at the thought. "Are you against carrying my bairns?"

"No, I am not."

"Then there will be no herbs. We will just... be careful when we couple."

"I feel tis not a good idea to rush these things."

"I can protect you, Orla, tis the only way."

"But we are talking about marriage, Brodie, and vows before God. Will you be able to keep those vows?"

"Aye."

Orla looked skeptical. "And what happens when a prettier woman comes along and she turns your head? What then?"

"There is no woman prettier than you, Orla."

It would seem Brodie had an answer for everything.

"Mayhap I should just marry Dalziel. If this is for my protection, it shouldn't matter if it's him or you."

"It does matter because I will kill Dalziel, then you will be a widow and have to marry me anyway," Brodie growled.

"Your sanity concerns me sometimes, Brodie."

Despite her misgivings, Orla could see the merit of his idea. There was no telling what the royal court could decide regarding her welfare. Macbeth could easily marry her off to a stranger if it benefitted a cause. But could she marry Brodie, knowing he would never *love* her?

"Come Orla, everyone is waiting. Trust me." He placed an arm around her shoulder.

Orla was going to concede, but thought about the rowan tree and all the women Brodie had been with over the years, and how that shattered her heart each time.

In horror, Orla realized she still loved Brodie. There was no way she could marry him and remain detached. It would only lead to heartbreak. Especially knowing he would never love her in return.

It was as if the rowan tree gave up its wisdom and warning, and Orla would heed it.

She pulled away from him. "I cannot marry you, Brodie, no matter what the future holds. I dinnae want to. It feels wrong."

Orla knew this because she wanted something more from a union with a man. She wanted love and *fidelity,* and they were things Brodie could never give her. At some point, he would get bored and he would move on to the next conquest. She would be alone again, mourning the loss of her old friend.

Protection was not a strong enough reason to marry.

It was Brodie's turn to tense at her words. Was she rejecting him? After everything he had done, she was throwing it back in his face. He felt so dejected. He got angry.

Brodie got in her face. "*Mo leannan*, we must do this. Why are you making this difficult?"

"Answer this question, Brodie. Why do you want to marry me?" Orla asked.

"To protect you, lass, I need to ken you're safe, and this is the only way to do it." He was now pacing the room.

"So, there is no other reason that compels you to marry me?"

Brodie stopped pacing and held her hands. "None stronger than the need to protect you."

Orla lowered her head and stared at the ground. Brodie's words confirmed the rightness of her decision. He felt nothing for her beyond protective instincts. He did not know how much she had loved him over the years. She doubted he even remembered anything from when they were children. Her future be damned. She would not let Brodie sacrifice his freedom for her. They would only end up fighting and bickering.

Orla pulled her hands free. "I cannot marry you for those reasons alone. I am sorry Brodie, but tis just not in me to bind myself to you like this."

Brodie clenched his jaw and stiffened at her words. "That's it then? No?"

"My answer is no."

Brodie only saw panic and anger melding as one. He did not realize how much he had been looking forward to binding Orla to him. It replaced his disappointment with anger.

"Is there someone else?"

"When would I have the time to be with someone, Brodie?"

"Let me see, in the woods today, when your lips were stuck to that blonde sponge cake."

"Twas just a kiss, Brodie."

"Is it just me you dinnae want, then?"

"Brodie, I dinnae want to marry *anyone* who only feels the need to protect me."

"Then I am sorry my offer was so disgusting to you, Orla. I shall withdraw it and you'll not hear it from me again." Brodies face shuttered, and he became distant.

"Brodie, I didn't mean—"

"I'll have someone else guard you tonight." Brodie stormed out of the room and slammed the door.

Orla felt the wet hit her cheek as she watched him leave. She felt bereft all over again. But she staunched the bleeding of her heart and told herself it was for the best. Better now than later when she became more attached.

Rejected

BRODIE WAS LIVID. HE had just poured his heart and soul out to the woman, and she rejected him. At the risk of her own life. If only he had kept his distance earlier, it would have saved him the trouble. What had his worthless father said to him all those years ago? *Never give your heart to a woman. She will tear your balls asunder.* Well, hello ripped balls.

Brodie arranged two guardsmen to see to Orla, then he went down to the chapel to notify the others that the wedding was canceled.

He did not expect an inquisition.

"What did you do, Brodie?" Dalziel asked.

"I did nothing!"

"You must have said something to upset her?" Beiste said.

"I am telling you, she didn't want to marry me. She rejected me."

"What did she say precisely?" Jonet asked.

"She asked me why I wanted to marry her, and I told her it was for her protection."

"And then?" Amelia asked.

"And then what?"

"Well, what other reason did you give her?" Amelia asked.

"Nothing, I just said, to protect her."

"Och, you daft fool," Morag piped in and smacked the top of his head.

"What did I do wrong?"

"Well, you make it sound like it's a chore to marry her," Sorcha replied.

"I did not mean it that way. I want to marry her with all my heart," Brodie said. Then looked surprised at his revelation.

"Then perhaps, son, you should have told her that," Abbot Hendry said.

Brodie cursed when he remembered her words. '*I dinnae want to marry anyone who only feels the need to protect me.*' They made sense now.

"Blast it! I'll be back," he said to the others and stormed out of the chapel. He needed to see Orla.

Brodie had just made it halfway across the Great Hall when the village bells started ringing. Two rings, a pause, then one ring, and a pause.

Brodie's entire body tensed because the signal meant one thing, *Raiders!*

Brodie changed direction, heading towards the armory, and almost ran straight into Morag.

She reached out and grabbed his arm in a death grip.

"Please move Morag, I dinnae have time!"

But he stilled when she spoke in an eerie voice. "Tis trickery, Brodie. The danger is in here."

Heeding her words, he ran towards his bed-chamber, sword drawn, only to find it empty. He cursed again.

Brodie wondered where Orla had gone, and he was angry that there were no guards at her door. He hoped like hell they were with her because he needed to organize the men and get to the village.

He grabbed his battle axe off the wall and flew downstairs to the bailey, where Dalziel and Beiste gathered with several hundred retainers.

Brodie told them of Morag's warning. They sent two-thirds of the men into the Village and woods with Dalziel and Beiste, while Brodie remained in the Keep with the rest. He gave orders to search the entire Keep for Orla and any threat within the Keep.

For Whom the Bells Toll

ORLA LOCKED THE DOOR after Brodie left and was sitting on the window nook staring out into the bailey. She felt despondent and maudlin. Why did she have to suffer unrequited love? It would be so easy just to give in and shackle herself to Brodie, but they would end up unhappy.

She stared out into the night and wondered about her parents. She wondered what type of people they were and worried about what awaited her at Dunsinane.

She was about to return to her bed when she saw a flash of light coming from the woods. She caught a responding flash coming from somewhere in the Keep.

She sat up. Whoever was out there in the forest, they were signaling someone inside. She blew out her candle and leaned further out the window to locate the signal. It was coming from the second floor of the guest wing.

Orla jumped up from the nook, quickly donned a pair of trews and tunic, and wore a dark hooded cloak. She put on her boots and placed a dirk inside one of them. She grabbed a dagger which was sheathed in a scabbard on her belt.

She opened the door and was surprised to find no one outside it. Not wanting to miss her opportunity, she ran across the landing and made her way down the stairs to the second floor.

Torstein and his men had quarters below and there were supposed to be guards patrolling the floor. But when Orla arrived, she found all the lights out and two guardsmen slumped on the ground unconscious. She bent down and checked their pulse. They were breathing. *Drugged.* Orla unsheathed her dagger and clutched it in her hand.

She checked the first three rooms and saw Torstein, Njal, and Mathias fast asleep. Orla wondered if they were drugged as well. She was moving towards the last door when she heard it click. Orla stepped into the shadows and stood with her back flat against the wall.

She saw a figure slinking past in the dark. It was Aksel. He was moving down the stairs. He had not spotted her.

Against her better judgment, Orla followed him.

She had just made it to the first floor when the village bells started ringing. Orla glanced out the window when something hard hit the back of her head. Then everything went black.

Cold Damp

ORLA OPENED HER EYES and winced in the dark. She tried to get her bearings despite the pounding in her head. Her hands were bound in front of her and she was sitting on the cold, damp stone floor. She shuddered at the memory of the last time she found herself on a cold, damp floor. She instinctively knew they were still in the Keep.

Her dagger was missing, but she could still feel the dirk hidden in her shoe.

"Lass ye made it so easy for me. Wandering aboot in the dark alone, I didn't have to find ye."

Orla saw Aksel standing in the doorway.

"Whatever you mean to do, you willna get away with it," she said.

"Och, but I already have." He moved closer.

Orla felt a ripple of fear.

"Everyone who can protect you is in the village searching for invaders. But the raider is here in the Keep." He chortled.

"You arranged the ringing of the bells?" Orla asked.

"Aye, twas easy. I paid a lad some coin and signaled to tell him when."

"What do you want with me?"

"I'm gan to kill you, but first I want to ken whit it's like to poke a jarl's *dattar* while she screams." He leered at her and raked his eyes over her chest.

Orla stiffened.

"Mayhap if I enjoy it, ah'll keep ye as me thrall." Aksel was standing over her now and rubbing his crotch.

"That's your plan?" Orla scoffed.

"Aye, whits wrong wid it." He scowled.

Orla burst out laughing. Maybe it was hysteria or the flashbacks she had being confined in a dark room. Her laughter sounded like a witch's cackle, and she could not stop.

Aksel backhanded her across the face. "Cease or I will kill ye now," he seethed.

Orla kept giggling. She pulled her knees up against her chest and leaned her head forward, chuckling and rocking back and forth.

Her hands moved fast towards her boot. She slid her fingers inside and gripped the handle of her dirk.

"I said stop laughing!" Aksel hissed. He pulled Orla to her feet. His focus was on her face and the need to wipe the smirk off it.

He had failed to notice that Orla now held a dirk in her hands. The blade tucked inwards against her bound wrists so he could not see.

Aksel stared at her, evil gleaming in his eyes. "I've changed me mind. I'm gan to kill ye now and then rut ye."

He pushed her up against the wall. Gripped her neck with his right hand and choked her. Then he raised his left arm, curled his hand into a tight fist, and aimed it at her face.

Orla remained calm as the world moved in slow motion. She kept her eyes on Aksel's left shoulder. As soon as it flinched, she swung her arms out to the side; the dirk gripped tightly in her bound hands. She twirled the blade away from her wrists and plunged it deep into the side of his rib cage. She pulled it out and gave him two more quick jabs to his side.

Aksel dropped his right arm and let go of her neck. Both hands went to his ribs as he staggered backward and struggled to breathe. She had punctured his lung.

Aksel looked down at the blood pouring from his side, and shock registered on his face. Then he glared at her with pure rage.

Orla knew men like Aksel, even severely injured, could be lethal.

She remembered feeling helpless when Ranalf groped her and beat her into unconsciousness. *No one would do that to her again.*

Without warning, Orla kicked Aksel hard in the groin. He buckled in pain and fell to his knees.

She bent down and whispered in his ear, "You said everyone who can protect me is in the village. But you forgot one person." Orla slammed the dirk down into the side of his neck. As the blood spurted onto her clothes she yelled— "Me!"

Then she removed the dirk and kicked him in the chest.

Aksel slumped to the floor, dead.

Breathing heavily and racked with exhaustion, Orla leaned back against the wall and slid down until her backside hit the floor. The dirk clattered to the ground beside her as she closed her eyes.

That was how Brodie found her moments later. Hands bound, covered in blood, and passed out on the floor.

Chapter 8 – You were Mine

There comes a time in every man's life when he has an epiphany. Orla was Brodie's revelation. When he stormed into the room and saw her covered in blood and passed out on the stone floor, he roared in anguish, thinking she was dead.

As he bent down to pick her up, he felt as if his heart were breaking.

But when Orla opened her eyes and said, "Brodie, will you stop bellowing? You're giving me a headache." He pulled her into his arms and wept in front of Rory and Lachlan. And he did not care one bit.

An hour later, the rest of the MacGregors had returned to the Keep after the false alarm and security was heightened. The young lad who had helped Aksel confessed that he was told he was helping the clan by ringing the bell.

It was discovered that Aksel had drugged several guards, including Torstein, Njal, and Mathias. Brodie had reprimanded the guardsmen for drinking during their shift.

The Keep eventually settled again as people sought their beds. The panic and excitement was over for another day.

Dalziel postponed the trip to Dunsinane, to give Brodie and Orla the opportunity to wed and the retainers a day's rest.

Brodie had yet to inform Orla of his wedding plans because he was busy helping her bathe and get ready for bed. She was too exhausted to argue.

It was just past midnight, and Orla was fast asleep in their bed. Brodie pulled her towards him, tucked her into his side, and wrapped his arms around her. He kissed her forehead and whispered the words he should have spoken to her when he asked her to marry him. "I love you, Orla."

Love Is A Battlefield

THE NEXT MORNING, THE Keep awoke to a war zone. The combatants were one reluctant bride-to-be and her kinswomen, and one overbearing bride-groom-to-be and his kinsmen.

"Orla, open this door right now or I'll kick it down," Brodie yelled.

"Do it. I hope you break a leg," Orla shouted in return.

"We are getting married today, and that's final," Brodie roared.

"I am not marrying you today or any day," she screamed.

Things had deteriorated between the couple since Orla had come down to the Great Hall for breakfast and heard Brodie invite everyone to their wedding.

It was the first Orla had heard of it. That lead to a screaming match on the dais which led to fruit and custard tarts being hurled from one side of the table to the other.

The altercation had ended with Orla, Amelia, and Iona locking themselves in Amelia's solar. While Brodie, Beiste (carrying baby Colban) and Dalziel threatened all kinds of retribution if they did not come out.

As with all highly emotional family disputes, members had taken sides, and a gridlock was being negotiated by a three-year-old girl.

"Uncle Brodie," Iona yelled. Interrupting the battle between Orla and Brodie.

"Aye, Sweeting," Brodie replied.

"Are you sick?"

"No, I'm not sick."

"Are you dying?"

"No, I'm not dying. Iona, please let me speak to Auntie Orla."

"Do you have the pox?"

"Iona—" Brodie said with exasperation.

"Mama says if men have the pox, they shouldna marry."

"Amelia, what the devil have you been teaching my child?" Beiste yelled.

"She's *our* child, Beiste, and she is just repeating what she hears. She does not ken what it means," Amelia retorted.

"Will someone open this bloody door?" Dalziel growled. "We have a Keep full of people waiting around. Someone is still trying to kill Orla, and we dinnae have time for this."

"All right." Orla sighed and opened the door.

The men filed into the solar except for Brodie, who just stood in front of Orla.

"What do you want, Brodie?" she asked.

"You, only you, and we are getting married right now." Brodie hauled her over his shoulder and marched her down to the chapel, ignoring her protests.

Beiste handed baby Colban to Amelia, then scooped her up in his arms and followed behind Brodie while Dalziel carried Iona down to the chapel.

When they reached the chapel, Morag, Jonet, and Sorcha were there to greet Orla.

Morag soothingly spoke to Orla. "Come now, child, dinnae fight fate."

Orla saw the truth of it. She finally relented, despite her misgivings that Brodie did not love her.

Amelia also relented and took Orla into a side chamber where Jonet and Sorcha had already prepared a wedding dress for her and a bouquet.

When Orla emerged, she looked resplendent in a long emerald, green kirtle and embroidered surcoat. The dress hugged her figure and accentuated her breasts. She wore her hair down and Amelia provided her with a fine handmade gold chain around her neck.

Orla entered the chapel, and it was full to overflowing with clan members.

As she walked down the aisle, she heard Iona gasp, "Auntie, you look like a faerie princess!"

Orla saw Abbot Hendry smiling at the center of the altar. Then she saw Brodie. He had also changed into his plaid with his family crest badge. His hair tied back, and he looked so handsome and eager to wed her. He gazed at her with want and need.

It reminded her of the way Beiste always looked at Amelia.

When Orla drew closer, Brodie reached out, pulled her to his side, and placed a gentle kiss on her cheek.

"Och, enough of that now. Wait until after the ceremony," Abbot Hendry huffed, and the congregation laughed.

The abbot began with the blessings. Then it came time for the vows.

Orla gave Brodie another chance to change his mind. "Brodie, you ken I can take care of myself. I am not yours to protect."

Brodie's response was swift. He looked down at her. His voice was firm and commanding. "You are wrong. You have always been mine, and I have every right to protect what belongs to me."

Brodie knew it was time to convince her, and in a loud voice, he began. "Orla, you were mine when you were six years old and came crying to me at the rowan tree because the others were teasing you."

Orla gazed at Brodie, astonished that he remembered.

"You were mine when you were seven and I belted the lads for locking you in the dungeons."

"Brodie..." Orla whispered, remembering the incident like it was yesterday. It was why she was afraid of dark places.

Relentless, he pushed on. "You were mine when you fell down the well at old man Mackenzie's farm and I took the whipping for you because he warned us not to go there."

Orla felt tears welling in her eyes as the flood of memories came back to her.

"You were mine when you were seven and a half and got lost in the caves because you were searching for faeries. I found you." Brodie wiped the tears from her eyes with his thumb as they fell.

"You were mine all the times you held my hand and sat with me after Da beat me."

"You were mine when you were seventeen and I ignored you because you were so pure. I did not want to sully you with the vile man I had become."

"And you were mine when you were eight years old and we handfasted in the woods, so you'd never be alone again."

Orla was astonished he remembered. She was shaking her head in disbelief.

Brodie said, "We agreed that day that if you were not married when I returned, I would marry you and be with you forever. That day has come *mo cridhe*."

Little did Orla know Brodie was about to shatter the walls of her resistance, removing the last barrier surrounding her fragile heart.

Brodie took her right hand and entwined it with his. "You are still mine and I am yours, only yours, from this day forward. The past is gone, there will be no others between us because… I 'Brodie the *Bear* Fletcher' take you 'Orla the *Huntress*' as my wife. I am yours and you are mine from this day to eternity."

"What are you doing?" Orla mumbled as she felt something slide against her wrist.

"Look at me, Orla. Say your vows, *mo leannan*, loud and clear." Brodie urged. His hand was held fast to her.

Orla spoke the words he longed to hear. "You are still mine and I am yours, only yours, from this day forward. The past is gone, there will be no others between us because I 'Orla the *Huntress*' take you 'Brodie the *Bear* Fletcher' as my husband. I am yours and you are mine from this day to eternity."

"Aye, tis done."

She turned and saw Abbot Hendry watching with a warm smile. "In the presence of God and witnesses, I now give you an official church blessing."

Orla looked down and noticed her hand was in Brodie's, but it was the tie that bound their wrists together that looked familiar. It was the same leather tie she had thrown over the cliff all those years ago. "But how?"

"I followed you that day when you left the rowan tree. I climbed down and retrieved it. I have kept it all these years."

"Why?" Orla asked.

"Because twas always my destiny to love you and for us to marry," Brodie replied.

"I have always loved you, Brodie Fletcher, and even more so today. Dinnae make me regret it," Orla whispered.

"Never."

The abbot made the sign of the cross, then said, "By the power invested in me, I now declare you husband and wife. You may kiss the bride."

Brodie did not hesitate. He wrapped his arms around Orla, pulled her close, bent his head, and gently kissed her lips. It was a chaste kiss, but when it was over, they both felt breathless. They stood for a moment, their faces mere inches apart, just smiling at one another, oblivious to the rest of the world.

And that was how Orla, the Huntress, and Brodie the Bear became man and wife. Standing in a chapel among friends and family. Their handfast became a legal and binding marriage, and there was not a single dry eye in the place.

None

AFTER A SMALL CELEBRATORY supper in Amelia's solar, Brodie and Orla finally retired to Brodie's spacious chambers, which had now become theirs. He carried her over the threshold and closed the door behind them.

Brodie placed her beside the bed and just gazed at her. She was the most beautiful woman he had ever beheld, and she was *his*. He wanted nothing more than to strip her naked out of that tempting dress. But Brodie was nervous. He had never been this nervous about coupling before.

The difference was, this was his *wife*, not some quick forgettable tup in the woods. This was Orla, the woman he *loved*. He needed their first time to be memorable for her. It had to be incredible. The type of lovemaking reserved for only the greatest lovers. Brodie needed to bring her to monumental heights of ecstasy and pleasure. It needed to be perfection.

But what if he could not satisfy her needs? What if she left him for that blasted Norse god?

The doubt set in.

Brodie decided he needed to kill Torstein first. He would get his sword go downstairs and slash a few cuts across that flawless face, so Orla never left him.

Brodie panicked at the thought that maybe he could not satisfy his wife. He started hyperventilating. His breathing became shallow. He was feeling faint. The room started spinning. His legs gave way. He sat on the bed, his elbows resting on his knees, his hands holding his head as he tried to take in deep breaths.

"Brodie! What is the matter? You look pale." Orla crouched down beside him. "Do you have a fever?" She felt his forehead. "You feel cold. Do you need some cider?" Orla rushed over to the table and poured a drink and shoved it towards him. "Here, drink this."

Brodie took a gulp, then started sputtering and coughing. "Cho... king... cannot... breathe."

Orla slapped his back. "I'll go get Amelia." Her voice was rising in panic.

"No," he said.

Orla knelt on the floor beside him. She took his face in her hands. "Brodie love, tell me what is wrong. What do you need me to do?"

Brodie glanced at Orla's concerned face. She looked as if she were about to weep, and all he saw was pure love shining back at him. The panic receded, and he calmed immediately, and with the calm came a ravenous hunger.

Orla was the one getting nervous now. Brodie had gone quiet, and he was staring at her like he was a lion, and she was a succulent piece of venison.

She stood and slowly backed away.

Brodie got to his feet and now towered above her.

"How many?"

"What?"

"How many men have you had?"

"I dinnae think that's—"

"How many lovers?"

"Brodie?"

"Tell me!" he roared.

"Dinnae yell at me, Brodie Fletcher!" she shouted.

He tilted his head, contemplating something. "Were they, my men?"

Orla gave him a wary look and folded her arms across her chest. "Why?"

"Because after I make love to you, I'm going to kill them for daring to touch what is *mine*!"

"Dinnae be ridiculous. If I were to do the same, for every woman you've swived, there would not be a female alive. If you dinnae want me because you think I am tainted, then—"

The distance between them vanished as Brodie grabbed her. "You misunderstand me. I need to ken if this is your first time. If not, then I willna be gentle because my need for you is fierce. So again—"

"None! You are my first," Orla blurted out. "So, I am not as well-practiced as you."

Brodie wanted to beat his chest and roar like a lion with the knowledge no other had claimed her. Even if she had been with others, it would have made no difference. He knew he had no right to hold her to standards he had not adhered to. But he would have hunted down every man and beat them to a pulp. Knowing that Orla was untouched meant he would be the one to introduce her to unimaginable pleasures, and that was a gift.

"Then. I. Will. Be. Your. First. And. Your. Last!" he said.

He took her in a passionate embrace. "Open your mouth," he growled.

Orla did, as his tongue sought entry to caress hers. Brodie deepened the kiss, holding her head in place so she could not back away. "Get rid of that dress now. I dinnae want to ruin it," he demanded and was panting, his eyes hooded.

Orla undid the emerald kirtle until it lay in a pool on the floor. She stood before him, wearing only her chemise.

Brodie grabbed both sides of the material and rend it in two.

She gasped. "That was my favorite chemise."

"I'll buy you a new one."

Orla's pert breasts were bared to his view. Her nipples hardened as they contacted the air. Brodie's eyes raked her body as he removed his leine and then his plaid. He stood before her, naked and gloriously aroused. His manhood jutted out thick, long, and hard.

Orla just stared at all that was Brodie and marveled at the wonder of her husband. Her body felt heated and positively wild. Her breathing was shallow with arousal. She licked her lips, and Brodie was undone.

Brodie said, "I will try to go slow and be gentle. Anytime you want me to stop or slow down or if you feel scared or anything you want to—"

"Oh, would you hurry up and stop talking, Brodie! I need you to claim me now! I trust you ken what to do and I will take your lead, but if you're going to spend the entire night blathering on—"

Brodie moved so fast, throwing Orla over his shoulder. He took two strides and tossed her onto the bed. "All right, you impatient minx. Dinnae say I didna warn you."

Brodie then lovingly gazed at every inch of her. When his eyes rested on her darkened areolas framed by light brown skin, his length hardened. His hand followed his eyes as he pinched a nipple. His pale hand was a stark contrast to her darker skin. *Mine!* Roared the possessive voice in his head.

Brodie bent over her left breast and began suckling her nipple. Orla moaned as he lavished attention on her breasts, his mouth alternating between them. His hand glided down to the juncture between her thighs, where she was slick and wet. He found her hooded pearl and applied pressure with his palm to cause the friction that had her moaning his name.

Brodie took in his beautiful wife. Her eyes were closed, her head thrown back, her hands gripping the sheets as she ground against his palm. He knew at that moment she was going to be a quick study as long as he took the lead.

"Aye, love, take your pleasure," he rasped.

At his seductive words, Orla stiffened and came. Brodie thought it was the most sensual thing he had ever witnessed.

He dropped to his knees beside the bed and kissed a path to her center. He spread her legs apart and laved her core twice with his tongue just to taste her. Satisfied that she was ready, he then stalked on all fours up the length of her body and lay on top of her, holding most of his weight on his forearms. He stared into her eyes and whispered. "I'm sorry I cannot take the time to do more, love. But I am fit to burst with the need to be inside you."

Orla smiled languidly at him. Some of his hair had escaped the hair tie. She tucked it behind his ear and spread her thighs wider to accommodate his hips. She reached down between them and caressed his hard length. With a husky voice, she whispered, "I love you, Brodie. I am yours."

Brodie removed her hand. "If you keep touching me, love, I willna last." He kissed her delectable lips and rubbed his cock between her moist core to lubricate his hard length. He was large, and he did not want to hurt her.

He could hear Orla gasping again as her hips thrust against his length, urging him to take her. She was becoming aroused. The most passionate lover.

Brodie could not wait any longer. He had waited years for this moment. Brodie placed the tip at her entrance. He stared into her eyes one more time to make sure she was all right. Orla nodded her head slightly and in one powerful surge; Brodie thrust his entire length to the hilt of her tight, slickened sheath.

Brodie groaned as Orla's heat enveloped him completely.

Orla stiffened, then started breathing in shallow gasps. Her arms wrapped tight around his torso; her hands gripped his shoulders as her hardened nipples rubbed against his chest.

Brodie stilled. "Are you alright, love?"

"Aye Brodie, I just feel so full. You are huge husband."

He kissed her and remained still, giving her body time to adjust. When he felt her relax, he raised a questioning brow. She blinked and nodded, then smiled.

Brodie groaned as Orla started tightening her inner core muscles, massaging his length internally as if trying to get used to the feel of him. She held a surprised look and gasped some more.

"Blast it, woman, I'm going to spill if you keep doing that."

Orla gave him a sultry smile and kept doing it; she whispered, "Then move, husband. I cannot do all the work."

Brodie needed no further encouragement as he began thrusting in and out of her. "Och, we'll see who does all the work, wife."

Their coupling became frenetic as Brodie moved harder and faster, seeking release. To his surprise, Orla matched his pace, grinding her hips in unison with his as grunts and moans reverberated around the chamber. Finally, their bodies stiffened as Orla came hard, raking her nails across his back. Brodie followed, roaring his pulsating climax to the night sky as he exploded inside her shuddering heat.

At Last

IN THE AFTERMATH OF their lovemaking, Brodie lay replete in his bed and utterly satisfied. Orla safely tucked into his side, her head resting against his chest. He could not keep his hands off her. Touching and grazing, kissing, caressing. The need to feel her beside him and touch her skin, drink in her scent was so strong.

Their first time together had been the best sex of his life, bar none. He felt their connection soul deep. It was not merely physical, but emotional.

What made it incomparable to any other encounter in the past was *love*. That was the key ingredient to curing his dissipation. Love for the woman in his arms, his wife. It could only get better from here.

"What are you thinking about, Wife?" Brodie loved the sound of that word.

"I was just wondering if you were happy with our coupling. I ken you have been with many women, and I just hope that I was—"

"You were the best I've ever had," he replied in all seriousness.

Orla's eyes softened.

"And what of me Orla, did I satisfy you?"

"Hmm, tis hard to say after only one time and I dinnae have any experience to compare it to. I will probably need a few more sessions to decide."

Brodie burst out laughing, which had Orla giggling.

"I jest, you were magnificent, Brodie," she said before planting a kiss on his chest.

"I meant to tell you beforehand you dinnae need to worry. I am clean," Brodie said.

"What do you mean?"

"Amelia insisted she check my manhood for diseases."

"She what?" Orla asked in shock.

"Aye, she has kept a keen eye on my health these past two years, and there was no way I could marry you if I carried an affliction."

"And Beiste, let her look at your manhood?"

"Aye, but he didn't like it. They had a screaming match over me. I dinnae understand how he can be married to a clan healer yet refuse to let her look at men's parts."

"Would you allow me to scrutinize other men's parts?" Orla asked.

"Not if you wanted every one of them dead," Brodie growled.

Orla burst out laughing. "Now you ken how Beiste feels."

"You ken I have not been with any other woman since Ranalf attacked you?" Brodie asked.

"But that was over two summers ago." Orla looked shocked.

"No need to tell me. I am the one who had blue balls for two summers. You ruined me for all others, Orla."

"You've been celibate all this time?"

"Aye."

"Brodie, you're lying. I saw you sneaking out of Zelda's cottage that night in the woods."

He shook his head. "That night I had given you up. You rarely gave me the time of day, and Beiste and Amelia were so protective of you. She was the first woman I sought, but it didn't work."

"What didn't work?"

"Little Brodie would not respond to her touch."

"Are you telling me you became impotent?"

"Aye. Nothing worked. I even tried to imagine you, but her scent was off, and no matter how much she caressed me with her ample bosoms, I felt even less excited."

Orla scowled and slapped his arm. "I dinnae need the details of her attempts, Brodie."

"Now who's jealous?" He raised a brow.

"But what of the tales of you wooing and seducing women every night?"

"Lies Orla. The last woman I shared a bed with for an entire night was you."

"What? When?"

"When you were recovering from Ranalf's attack. I used to sneak into your bed and sleep beside you when the night terrors came. After that, it became a habit. I often snuck into your bed at night. Morag even caught me once and said nothing."

"I wonder why Ma said nothing."

"Mayhap she kenned I was changing," Brodie replied. "The night I found you unconscious was the night everything changed for me. I refused to leave your side, no matter how many times Amelia tried to shoo me away. I would often just sit and watch you sleep."

"That sounds very..."

"Romantic?"

"No, disturbing."

"Och, you never complained. In fact, you could barely keep your hands off me, you saucy wench." He winked at her.

"I was half delirious, Brodie. I did not have the strength to fight off a randy brute." She huffed.

Brodie chuckled. "You keep telling yourself that, love. I ken how obsessed you are with my braw body."

With that, Orla picked up her pillow and hit him with it.

Brodie grabbed the pillow and pulled her towards him. What began as a tussle over a pillow soon turned into a tussle within the sheets.

It was a battle Brodie won when it ended with him coming violently inside his new wife shortly after her fingernails scorched his butt cheeks as she screamed her release.

Last Name

THE NEXT DAY, THE KEEP was busy with the travel contingent getting ready to head to Macbeth's castle in Dunsinane.

Brodie had spent the night gently introducing Orla to the pleasures of passion. He knew she would be tender after their first time and showed her other ways to seek satisfaction which meant she was a little fatigued. Brodie, much to her annoyance, was full of energy.

He had warm baths drawn for them and breakfast ready for her when she woke.

It was after their bath when they were breaking their fast together, wearing nothing but towels, that Brodie surprised Orla with a parcel. When she opened it, it contained several richly woven garments made of fine wool and colorful linen, including court slippers.

Orla looked at the clothing in awe.

"What is this?"

"Tis some clothes for you to wear at Court."

"They are beautiful, but where did you get these?"

He blushed slightly, and Orla became suspicious.

"Brodie Fletcher, dinnae tell me these clothes are from one of your past lovers." She scowled.

"No! They were made just for you."

"How? When? These would have cost many coins..."

"I asked the clan seamstress to make them for you."

"And she made all these last night?" Orla looked skeptical.

Brodie blushed again. "She made them last summer."

Orla looked confused. "I dinnae understand?"

"I had them made for you last summer. She already had your measurements, so I chose some material and colors I thought would suit you."

"Why last summer?"

"I had decided, at least hoped, that someday we would marry, and I wanted you to have nice things." Brodie shrugged his shoulders and looked embarrassed by the confession.

Orla stilled and stared at Brodie. "You have wanted to marry me since last summer?"

"Aye."

"That tis... that tis... the loveliest thing I have ever heard," Orla replied before she burst into tears.

"Och, lass dinnae cry." Brodie crossed the distance between them, picked her up, and settled her on his lap. "Shh love, tis alright now... dinnae cry."

Orla just buried her face in his neck and wrapped her arms around him.

"I love you, Brodie Fletcher," she said between intervals of hiccups.

"I love you too, Orla Fletcher," he replied.

Orla raised her head and whispered with reverence, "I have a last name."

"Aye, you do."

"I finally have a last name. You gave me a last name."

She stared at her husband with such an outpouring of love, eyes rimmed with tears. Brodie felt as if his heart was going to explode, trying to contain it all.

He held his breath, wondering if she was going to ball again. Instead, Orla shocked him when she grabbed his head and kissed him. She then climbed him like a tree, straddling his thighs and grinding herself against him.

"I need you now, husband. I cannot wait. Get this cloth off!" she shouted while trying to pull his towel away.

Brodie groaned. He was instantly hard watching his wife turn into a crazed she-cat. He did as she asked and released his hard length into the open air.

He pulled her cloth away, exposing her flushed heat to his. They were kissing with wild abandon when Orla leaped off his lap and knelt between his thighs. She pumped his stiff length twice with her hand before Brodie felt her hot, wet mouth engulf his length. Brodie groaned and threw his head back as Orla suckled and lavished him with her tongue.

Then, just as quickly, she released him with a popping sound, stood, and straddled him. She placed him at her center and lowered her body, allowing his length to stretch her inner walls until he was seated to the hilt.

Brodie held her hips and could barely breathe. He heard her low moan as he began thrusting in and out of her heat. She rode him in return, grinding down to meet his upward thrusts. Her breasts bounced mere inches from his face as he pounded into her. He lowered his mouth and latched on, suckling her nipples. Brodie dug his fingers into her buttocks, keeping her in place as she rode him hard.

It was a fast, frenzied coupling. The kind he had never experienced before.

They built their need to a crescendo and exploded at the same time. He roared when her contractions set off his climax, and he swallowed her scream with a passionate kiss.

Orla collapsed onto his chest, both still on the chair, breathing hard.

Once they caught their breath, Brodie said, "Remind me to buy you garments more often, love."

They burst out laughing.

Chapter 9 – To Dunsinane

An hour later, Brodie had packed their belongings. Readied their horses and seen to his guardsmen.

One thing Orla was discovering about her new husband, he was organized, efficient, and practical. He also anticipated her needs.

Before she asked, Brodie informed her he found her bow, quiver, and dagger. He also had her dirk cleaned and sharpened. Her weapons were sitting beside the window.

It was the strangest predicament for someone who was used to fending for herself. She only hoped that she could be of help to him in return.

By the time Orla went downstairs, fifty MacGregor retainers gathered in the bailey. The contingent included Dalziel and Brodie. Torstein, Njal and Mathias.

Beiste and his family would remain at the Keep with his War Band, as there was much work needed to secure their land against raiders.

Amelia was the only person unhappy with this arrangement. She felt she needed to accompany Orla as it also gave her a chance to visit Macbeth and his wife, Queen Gruoch. Macbeth was Amelia's second cousin.

But Beiste had refused to place Amelia in danger and would not allow his wife to "Hie off across the Highlands without him." Those were his exact words.

When they were ready to leave, a crowd gathered to bid farewell.

Amelia hugged Orla and handed her a parcel of healing herbs and salves should she need it.

Morag also handed Orla a parcel. It contained an intricately embroidered doll. A soft toy for a little girl.

"Um... thank you?" That was all Orla could say as she stared at it in confusion.

Morag just shrugged her shoulders. "I dinnae ken it either, lass, but best ye take it all the same. Someone needs it."

Orla had learned over the years to take whatever gift Morag offered, no matter how confusing.

She tucked the packages into her side bag and got ready to mount.

When they left the Keep, they set a fast pace. Dalziel had given them three days to get to Dunsinane, and it was safer to travel fast and light instead of dallying on the road.

Orla rode surrounded by retainers while Brodie sent scouts ahead on each leg of the journey.

It was the first time Orla had witnessed Brodie at work. He was impressive, and it made her proud that he was her husband. He was adept at his job, and she trusted him with her life.

A House

THE GROUP SET A RELENTLESS pace, with only a few rest stops. Mainly for the benefit of their horses. When they rested, Orla sat close to Brodie. He was forever shadowing her wherever she went.

That night, the contingent camped by *Loch Earn* just outside of *St Fillans*. It was while they were sharing a meal of fresh salmon and oatcakes Orla had prepared that Brodie broached the subject of living arrangements.

"What do you mean, where will we live? In my cottage, where else?" Orla said.

"I was thinking maybe we should live in my home, now that I have someone to share it with."

"Your family home?" Orla asked. Thinking about the run-down cottage where Brodie's father used to live. She was already calculating in her head the number of repairs it needed and what materials she could purchase to make it livable.

"No, I meant our home, on my land."

"You have land?" she asked, shocked.

"Aye, I have an estate and a large house. Tis run by a housekeeper and her husband. They maintain it while I have been at the Keep."

"But how?"

"Through my ma's *father*. She came from landed yeomen. It passed to me as the only surviving male heir."

"And you did not want to live there before?" Orla asked.

"I did not want to live there alone. But now I have a wife and... possibly bairns. I think we should move there."

Orla was wondering if she knew Brodie at all. He had a large house and land with workers?

"Where-ever you are, *is* my home, Brodie Fletcher," she said.

"Good answer, Orla Fletcher." Brodie smiled and kissed her.

Satisfaction

ON THE SECOND DAY OF their journey, Orla rode alongside Torstein.

Torstein expressed his regret that they had not protected her against Aksel.

"I should have kenned he was too eager to join us for this mission," Torstein said.

"Dinnae fash yourself, Tor. He did not harm me. Had you kenned him long?" Orla asked. Hoping that Torstein would not grieve for a close friend.

"Two summers. He gained our trust quickly, but I ken now he *mis* have been spying for Rognvald all that time."

"How long have you kenned Njal and Matthias?"

"Since we were boys," Matthias piped in.

"Aye, I trust them with my life," Torstein said. "Njal was wary of Aksel from the beginning, but I didn't listen to him." Torstein looked regretful.

"Aye, no one ever listens to small men," Njal said in a rumbly voice.

Given that Njal was the largest man she had ever seen, Orla wondered if he was serious until she saw him grinning.

"I wish ye well on yer marriage, peedie bird," Torstein said.

"Thank you." Orla smiled at him.

"Aye, twas a beautiful service. I had tears when yer husband spoke of your hand-fast," Njal said in all seriousness. "I damn near wept like a babe."

"The vows were vera poetic. Yer husband should be a bard," Matthias smirked.

Orla chuckled.

"If ye change your mind and your husband doesna satisfy ye, come to me and I'll show ye how a real man cares for his woman," Torstein said with a grin.

Before Orla could respond, Brodie and his destrier forced their way in between them.

"I satisfy my wife all the time, especially when I make her scream with pleasure!" Brodie replied while glaring at Torstein.

Orla groaned with embarrassment.

Torstein stifled a laugh. It was so easy to rile the brute; he thought.

Two Blades

AFTER ANOTHER DAY'S hard ride, they stopped for the night by the *River Tay* in *Perth*. It was during this time the men relaxed while some trained and sparred together.

While Brodie was walking the campsite, seeing to his guardsmen, Orla sat on a tree stump watching Dalziel train with his daggers. She was in awe. She had watched him spar with others before and he was light on his feet but deadly.

Noticing he had an audience, Dalziel said, "You did well, protecting yourself against Aksel, with your dirk, but I can teach you how to work with two blades if you wish."

Orla jumped at the opportunity.

They spent the next hour sparring with daggers as Dalziel gave her lessons in self-defense.

"Breathe, Orla," he said. "Clear your mind. The knives must become a part of you, an extension of your body. The way you become one with your bow is the same with blades. However, in close combat, these are more effective."

Dalziel stood directly behind her and grabbed her neck. Holding firm. "Now use the knives to get out of my hold. Dinnae worry about hurting me. Use everything you've got."

Orla counterattacked. Slashing behind her, but Dalziel was faster. He twisted his body away each time and blocked her blade with his own.

His skill level impressed Orla.

"Use your back, your buttocks as I taught you," he said.

Orla used her bottom to jerk back against his hips to escape his hold. It was working.

That was how Brodie found them. Bodies connected and out of breath.

"What's this?" Brodie growled.

"Training. Orla needs a lot more of it," Dalziel replied, releasing her.

"Why did you not ask me to help you train, Orla? I am good with knives." Brodie sulked.

Dalziel snorted.

"I am!" Brodie glared at Dalziel.

"Husband, if I need lessons in wielding an axe, I ken you are the best, but you have to agree, Dalziel is better with daggers."

"Mayhap Dalziel and I will need to have a session?" Brodie folded his arms across his chest and challenged Dalziel.

"No, Brodie, you will not cut into my training time." Orla scowled at him.

"Fine, but you better keep your randy hips away from my wife's ass, Dalziel." Brodie walked past Dalziel and made a 'V' sign with his first two fingers. He pointed them at his own eyes and then at Dalziel. Then silently mouthed, "I'm watching you."

Dalziel mouthed, "Fuck off," in return.

Mercenaries

IT WAS ON THE THIRD day when they were set upon just outside of *Scone* in the province of *Gowrie*.

Brodie knew this last stretch would be the most treacherous. Viking invaders came across the *North Sea* and used the *River Tay* as an entryway to the heart of Scotland.

The contingent had just stopped to water the horses. Fortunately, they were already on high alert. When the attack came, Brodie pushed Orla behind him and blocked an enormous fist from hitting him in the face.

Concern for Orla spurred him on as several men came running out of the woods.

Brodie roared, reached behind him, pulling out his square head battle axe strapped to his back. He swung it at his attacker, severing the man's arm. He spun his axe around and used the blade to prevent another attacker's sword from aiming for his chest. Then Brodie twirled his axe again, angling it at another man's thigh, slicing deep to the bone. Brodie used the handle to block yet another attacker's blade.

Orla stood in awe of her husband. His body shielded her as he dispatched one man after another with his battleaxe. She had never seen a large man move so fast with such graceful, effortless movements. He anticipated his aggressor's every move, which cost them their lives.

No matter how many men came at him, no matter what kind of weapon they wielded, Brodie did not flinch or hesitate. Instead, she watched as her husband methodically cut a path of destruction through the sea of men.

Orla took mental notes that she was definitely going to take battle axe lessons from him.

It relieved Brodie to see Orla keeping out of danger.

He knew the others had formed a circle around her. He saw Torstein and his men engaged in combat, and their fighting abilities impressed him.

Brodie saw Dalziel putting his daggers to good use. Dalziel was lightning fast. His victims did not know they had been cut. Brodie watched the shock on the faces of men, their swords raised, looking down in horror as their intestines spilled onto the ground. Meanwhile, Dalziel had already moved on to his next victim.

Scanning the surrounding area, he saw most of his men were engaged in combat and they were winning.

Whilst taking stock of his men, Brodie was momentarily distracted and had not realized Orla was no longer behind him.

Two attackers surged forward, taking Brodie by surprise. One of them threw a small axe at him. Brodie had just enough time to deflect it from lodging in his shoulder. But he was too slow to stop the second attacker from barreling into his side and knocking him to the ground. The force winded him.

His opponent stood over him and swung his blade to deliver a killing blow. But before he could, an arrow pierced the man's neck and then another his chest. He stumbled backward and fell down dead.

Brodie looked in the arrow's direction and his heart lodged in his throat when he saw his wife balancing on the branch of a tall tree. She was shooting arrows from the sky. Her aim was true every time.

If Brodie were not angry, he would have been proud.

By the end of the skirmish, the bodies of the dead attackers numbered thirty-seven. The MacGregors only registered a few minor injuries.

Once Brodie pulled Orla out of the tree, (the two of them arguing the whole time, much to the amusement of everyone watching) she used her parcel of healing herbs and bandages to see to everyone's wounds.

Dalziel interrogated one of the injured survivors. He said they were mercenaries hired by a man called, "One-hand."

King Macbeth's Castle, Dunsinane Hill, Perthshire

IN THE PAST MONTH, Macbeth mac Findlaích 'The Red King,' had received four urgent missives from four different parties all pertaining to the same matter.

One was from an ex-guardsman, Hagan Alfsson of Orkney. Another missive was from Chieftain Beiste MacGregor. The third was from Moddan of Caithness. But it was the fourth parchment which caused him the greatest amount of confusion, for it came from an Emissary to the Queen of Abyssinia.

Macbeth had traveled the globe extensively. He had a wealth of wisdom and expertise in battles. They called him 'The Red King' because of his ability to turn battlefields red with blood. But Macbeth's actual power came from his acumen for political strategy and manipulating events to his advantage. Yet in all his years of maneuvering, he had never come across an issue as complicated as this.

His wife, Queen Gruoch came to stand beside him. "What is it, my love? You have been frowning over those parchments for close to an hour."

"Tis a bizarre matter involving Jarl Thorfinn's *nighean*," he replied as he pulled her onto his lap and kissed her cheek.

"I did not ken cousin Thorfinn had a daughter?" she said.

"Aye, and according to these papers, neither does he."

Macbeth sensed that a day of reckoning was coming. He had to find his cousin. He just hoped that once he did, Thorfinn would not kill them all.

Chapter 10 – Macbeth's Castle

Dunsinane, Scotland

The MacGregor contingent reached Birnam Wood. Just beyond stood Macbeth's fortified castle on Dunsinane Hill. Its grey stone exterior and ominous presence were like a Leviathan rising from the depths of the sea, eager to devour its prey.

Orla had been here once before when Amelia was called before the Commissary to defend charges brought against her. It was a perilous journey then, as it was now. Orla, too, wondered what fate awaited them beyond the castle walls.

When they arrived, they were taken to their rooms in the guest quarters.

As they walked down the hallway, a voluptuous red-headed woman greeted Brodie and touched his arm. "Brodie?" she said in a sultry voice.

Brodie instantly removed her arm from his and said, "Please keep your hands to yourself."

"Come now, ye never worried where my hands went before." She gave him a lascivious smile.

"Well, I do now that I have a wife." He pulled Orla to his side.

The woman flinched and stepped away. "I beg yer pardon."

Orla knew there was no escape from Brodie's past indiscretions. *Was there no woman on the planet who had not been intimate with her husband?* She sighed.

"A past acquaintance?" Orla raised her eyebrow.

"Aye, Jocelyn or... Janice..."

"You dinnae even remember her name, do you?"

"No. As you said, she's in the *past*. You are my present and my future."

Brodie urged Orla forward and attempted to distract her. "Look at that tapestry, love! Is that not the largest tapestry you have ever seen? Tis amazing, the fine detail and all those bright colors..."

Orla just shook her head and chuckled.

Truth

LATER IN THE EVENING, Brodie, Dalziel, Torstein, and Orla were summoned into King Macbeth's private study. This was a privilege as very few entered the King's private wing.

It surprised Orla to see how relaxed Brodie and Dalziel were in the King's presence. It was as if they knew each other well.

She and Torstein were the only ones who seemed nervous.

"Come sit, my dear." Macbeth ushered Orla into the room and pulled out a chair for her. He then ushered everyone else to be seated around the table. "Now then, what do we have here?" Macbeth turned to Torstein. "Torstein Hagansson, you are Hagan Alfsson's son," Macbeth said as a statement, not a question.

"Aye yer majesty." Torstein nodded reverently.

"And your family shared the unenviable task of protecting Orla all these years," Macbeth stated.

"Aye," Torstein replied.

"I believe my humble thanks are in order," Macbeth said.

Torstein nodded in acknowledgment.

Macbeth turned to Orla with a warm smile. "Now then, my dear cousin, let us see if we can understand your predicament."

Macbeth turned once more to Torstein and said, "I received a missive from your da and I think tis safe now to tell us the full truth."

The others looked confused. They assumed Torstein had divulged everything he knew.

To their surprise, Torstein replied, "Aye, Your Majesty." He then shared the tale from the beginning.

"My *mor* Runa was a lady's maid at Thorfinn's stronghold. The jarl had gone away to see to matters in Caithness and Norway when his thrall, Izara, went into early labor.

"Thorfinn loved Izara to the point he planned to make any male child of their union his heir. No one cared much until they discovered Izara was with child.

"If she had a boy, there would be issues over territorial succession. A male could affect Brusi and Einar's share. They were Thorfinn's half-brothers.

"When Orla was born there *wis* great relief. A girl could not claim any title. The threat was gone."

"Then why was I sent away?" Orla asked.

"Aye, why send her away when she was no longer a threat?" Dalziel asked.

Torstein replied, "If it wis just ye, then there would not have been any trouble. But it wis not just you."

"What do you mean?" Brodie asked.

"A few minutes after Orla wis born, Izara labored again."

"But how?" Orla asked before realization hit.

"Twins," Dalziel, Brodie, and Macbeth replied in unison.

"Aye, twins. You had a brother and relief turned to fear," Torstein said.

Orla slumped in her chair, rocked by the revelation. "I had a brother?"

Torstein replied, "Aye, your brother's entry into the world changed everything. With the love Thorfinn had for your *mor*, he would have made his son his heir and petitioned for greater territories.

"The other earls of Orkney, Einar, and Brusi decided ye all had to die.

"Rognvald, Brusi's son, was in Norway with the king and ensured Thorfinn was delayed while Einar sent men to do his bidding. Your *mor* fought off the attackers, but she couldn't stop the fire."

"Then how did Orla survive?" Dalziel asked.

"The fire had engulfed everything so quickly Izara could only save one child. She gave Orla to my *mor* Runa."

The room went silent until Macbeth finally spoke. "I have sent men to find Thorfinn. In the meantime, ye will all remain as my guests until I receive word. I suspect there is far more to this tale than we can ever imagine."

"Should we not just arrest Rognvald at least to bring him to justice until Thorfinn arrives?" Brodie asked.

"No, I cannot do that. I dinnae have jurisdiction over the Orkney Isles. They are a province of Norway. Only their king can bring down such an edict and tis unlikely he will," Macbeth replied.

"What if ye invaded and expanded your territories?" Dalziel asked.

"Och, tis not possible. Only Thorfinn can seek justice in that region. His father Sigurd was the Norse earl before him, and his mother was King Malcolm's daughter. Only he can take out Rognvald without causing a war between Scotland and Norway."

Macbeth was quiet for a while, then said, "I suggest we keep things between us. For now, ye are just Mrs. Fletcher from the MacGregor clan and my special guest, given my connection to Amelia MacGregor."

Orla nodded, but heard little else. She wept quietly at the heartache of knowing her mother fought hard to save her bairns.

Brodie scooped her up and placed her onto his lap. He then held her close.

That night in their private guest-chamber, Brodie held her as she wept and comforted her in her sorrow. Orla knew as long as she had Brodie by her side. She could weather any tempest.

Market Day

THE FOLLOWING DAY, while Brodie was in talks with Dalziel and the king, Queen Gruoch ingen Boite, invited Orla to share a meal in her private quarters.

The two women had met previously when Orla had accompanied Amelia to the Castle two summers ago. Orla found Queen Gruoch to be an intelligent woman with a friendly disposition. She also loved children and for the first hour, Orla fielded constant inquiries about how Amelia's bairns, Iona, and Colban were getting on.

"How are you finding life at Court?"

"Tis most comfortable, Your Majesty."

"Please, there is no need to stand on ceremony. Call me Gruoch. Tis what my husband's kin call me when we are in private quarters."

"Aye, thank you, Gruoch, you have been most kind to me."

"I think today we need an outing to lift your spirits, Orla. I propose we head to the village of *Collace* tis Market Day today and there is always fine fare."

"I would love to, but is it safe?"

"I will take my guardsmen and we can take some of yours. Come now."

An hour later they set off to the village with royal guards and several MacGregor retainers, who stayed close as the women talked.

Queen Gruoch wanted to know everything about Orla's life, including how she ended up married to the braw Brodie Fletcher. The Queen was a hopeless romantic and sighed several times as Orla recounted her life's story.

When they reached the marketplace, the Queen had stopped to speak to a silk merchant when Orla noticed a familiar face manning a pottery stall nearby.

She was about to greet him when he interrupted her.

"Dinnae say a word, lass. Pretend ye dinnae ken who I am. Keep looking at the wares." He spoke in a hushed tone as he continued to bustle around his stall.

Orla was surprised because it was Malise Maclean, Amelia's uncle from the Isle of Mull in the Hebrides. He was a laird. She wondered why he was at a pottery stall looking like a merchant and in Dunsinane, of all places.

Orla kept looking at the pots with the pretence of talking more.

"What is happening?" she whispered.

"There is much treachery at Court. Dinnae trust anyone, least of all One-Hand," Malise replied as he scribbled something on a piece of paper.

"Who?"

"Best ye ask, Dalziel," he replied.

Orla heard someone approaching.

Malise cleared his throat and said in a loud voice, "Och now, lass, that there is a good sturdy jar for salves. Why dinnae ye take it as a gift?" Malise held out a jar for her.

Orla knew to follow his cue. "Aye, this will do nicely. But I insist on paying."

"Tis free for a bonnie lass like ye." Malise winked.

Orla saw a piece of parchment inside the tiny jar. She pocketed it in her surcoat and thanked Malise.

At that moment, one of the Queen's guardsmen appeared at her side and said, "Come, we must keep moving."

Later that afternoon, while Orla was in the guest-chamber of the castle. She took out the note from the jar and read the words, "Beware of Moddan."

Riddles

ON THE FOURTH DAY OF their stay at Dunsinane, Dalziel sat beside Orla in the Great Hall as they partook of their noon-day meal.

"Do you love Brodie?" he asked her.

"With all my heart," she replied.

"Would you do anything to protect him?"

"I would."

"Even if it means giving him up?"

Orla stiffened. "What do you mean?"

"Sometimes in life, people need to sacrifice for the ones they love."

"Dalziel, what are you saying?" she was getting a bad feeling.

"I need to make sure that what you feel for Brodie is genuine love, because if it is not then let him go."

"You're scaring me Dalziel, why the riddles?"

"I am just saying, given your recently elevated status, there may be a time when things will have to change."

Orla knew Dalziel was forewarning her, but she knew not about what.

"Dalziel tell me the truth dinnae bandy about words."

Dalziel looked wistful. "That is the problem, Orla. I wear so many faces, see so many things, I dinnae ken what the truth is anymore."

"Has the king said something?"

Dalziel stood abruptly. "I must go. Stay close to Brodie and trust that I will do all I can to protect you both."

With that Dalziel disappeared down the hall.

Orla suddenly lost her appetite.

Chapter 11 – Thorfinn 'the Mighty' Jarl of Orkney

The Atlantic Ocean

Seaspray lashed across Thorfinn Sigurdsson's face as he inhaled icy air deep into his lungs. He felt invigorated every time he crossed the Atlantic.

Thorfinn cut a threatening figure standing tall at 6 ft 9, wielding his sword and golden spear. He stood on the deck of his sixteen *rúm*, thirty-two rower *snekkja*. The swiftest warship in the sea. Open to the elements with speed and maneuverability.

As the infamous Jarl of Orkney, he raided lands and ruled the seas with blood and violence.

Lucky in battle and skilled in war. They did not call him 'Thorfinn the Mighty' for nothing. Not even nature dared to stand in his way as the dragon head *snekkja* sliced through icy waters.

Its destination Norway.

Thorfinn had a new king. A boy had ascended the throne. They called him 'Magnus the Good.'

Thorfinn wanted only one thing from this new king... *Orkney*.

King Magnús Óláfsson's Castle - Norway

KING MAGNUS 'THE GOOD' addressed Thorfinn. He was only nineteen summers old and already a powerful king of Norway and Denmark.

His physique and wisdom made him seem much older than his age.

"I know why you have come, Jarl Thorfinn," Magnus said.

"Your Majesty, I want *whit* is rightfully mine. I request dominion over the Isles," Thorfinn replied.

"You speak as if you own the Orkneys. It is but a province of Norway and my *Far*, King Olaf saw fit to divide the ruling share. You have enough."

Thorfinn clenched his jaw. "Tis never enough. I have raided and pillaged Alba and the Hebrides so all the riches could return to Norway. I did all this without the aid of my half-brothers or their sons."

"No, you raided these lands to build riches for yourself. I am not blind to the number of ships you now sail," Magnus replied with nonchalance.

Thorfinn was losing patience. "Need I remind ye, yer coffers are full because of *my* warships? I have brought five *kaupskips* full of riches. Consider it a gift."

Magnus changed the subject. "I hear you are to marry soon. My congratulations. Ingibiorg Finnsdottir is my cousin. I trust you will be kind to her."

"Aye, she is a gentlewoman, and she will provide me with fine sons," Thorfinn replied.

"Did you know her uncle was partly responsible for my *Far's* death?"

Thorfinn refrained from rolling his eyes. He knew where Magnus was heading with this. "Aye. Tis a pity one cannot choose their family members."

There was silence. Thorfinn knew his fiancé's uncle would become a bone of contention with the Norwegian king, but there was nothing he could do.

Magnus said, "I thank you for the gifts, but I have decided Rognvald, your nephew, will remain ruler of the Shetlands. He fostered here with my family and I will not take away his territorial rights."

Thorfinn just gritted his teeth. Denied again. His mind was already ticking. He would find another way to rule. Thorfinn nodded to the King and was turning to leave.

"Where do you travel now?" Magnus asked.

"I go to see my cousin Macbeth. Tis a surprise visit. I have much to discuss with him about matters in Alba."

"May I come with you? I would like to meet this... king of Alba."

It annoyed Thorfinn. The last thing he wanted was a boy tagging along, getting into his business. "Aye, Your Majesty. We leave on the morrow's morn if it pleases ye."

Royal Palace, Lake Hayq, Wollo Province, Abyssinia

QUEEN GUDIT SAT IN the throne room, reflecting on her long life. She was tired... so tired. She had now reigned sovereign for over forty years, keeping her enemies at bay for most of her rule and destroying anyone who stood in her way.

It was hard work being a queen.

"Ha!" she scoffed when she remembered something funny. Then her smile disappeared as she looked out across the desert plains.

It had been twenty-four years since she lost Izara.

In the beginning, her scouts had followed several leads, but with her nation occupied with wars of its own, the trail went cold.

Now, there was only one last piece missing.

Gudit heard a commotion outside before the doors burst open and her grandson, Kato, strolled in.

Zenabu, her advisor, followed behind him, grumbling. "My *li'uli*, I need to announce you to the Queen."

"There's no need to announce me, Zenabu. I think she can see I am here." Kato grinned as Zenabu just shook his head and made a '*tsk*,' sound.

Kato walked straight to his grandmother. Kissed her on the cheek and seated himself beside her. Breaking all protocol.

Gudit let him get away with it because he was her favorite grandson, and he knew it.

He was a handsome man, tall, broad, and strong. He would make a great king someday. She thought. If only his skin was not so fair. The nobles would not question his right to the throne.

Gudit cursed his sire again. If she ever got her hands on that Norseman, she would kill him.

"*Seti ayati* I have news," Kato said.

She smiled and asked, "What is it?"

"Master Ajani has found her."

Gudit inhaled sharply and felt the tears well in her eyes. Finally, the missing piece.

Chapter 12 – Brood of Vipers

Collace Village Inn, Perthshire, Scotland

Three monks sat quietly in the *Collace* Village Inn. They paid good coin for a table in the back room, away from rowdy punters. Each arrived separately and alone. Keeping their hooded robes on to conceal their faces. They spoke in hushed tones and in Latin.

From a distance, they looked like humble men of the monastic order, seeking a quiet place to break their journey.

Little did the patrons know the men were anything but monks. In fact, one was Macbeth, the king of Scotland, the other, Laird Malise Maclean from the Hebrides, and the third was Dalziel Robertson, a part Scottish Northumbrian Thane.

Dalziel said, "There were two men sent to kill Orla. One was Vidar, the other a Samuel from Northumbria. He called me the Wolf as if he kenned who I was."

"Where is he now?" Macbeth asked.

"A place he can never return from."

"Good. One less loose tongue in the world. Do you ken who sent him?" Macbeth asked.

"Aye, the earl of Shetland."

Macbeth was contemplative for a while then said, "Tell me of this attack outside of *Scone*."

Dalziel replied, "I interrogated one survivor, and he said, '*One-hand*' sent them."

"Damn, that man is everywhere. He is becoming a real menace, especially in the Hebrides," Malise replied.

"What do you mean?" Macbeth asked Malise.

"One-hand sided with raiders and leads many of the attacks. He says it's for the king of Alba."

Macbeth looked at both men before cursing. "Damn these Norsemen. They are the bane of my existence."

"What do you mean?" Dalziel asked.

Macbeth slumped into his chair. "There's something you both should ken."

Dalziel stiffened. Malise sat up straighter.

"One-hand is *my* man, and he is here in Dunsinane," Macbeth replied.

"He's here?" Malise asked in shock.

Dalziel stood abruptly, then sat down again, realizing he needed to keep up their ruse. Instead, he clenched his fists. "What do you mean?"

"Calm. Let me explain."

Dalziel nodded.

"His name is 'Moddan.' He is my assassin in *Caithness* and the Orkneys. He kens who you are, Dalziel, and tis likely this Samuel got wind of your identity through him."

"With respect, Your Majesty. Why did you send *your* man to kill Orla?" Dalziel clenched his jaw.

Macbeth replied, "That is precisely my point. I did not send him to kill anyone. I did not even ken he's raiding the Hebrides in my name." Macbeth tapped his index finger on the tabletop to emphasize his point. "His job was to watch and gather information, that is all. Which means I can no longer trust him, but I cannot extract him without alerting suspicion about other matters."

"Fuck!" Dalziel whispered.

Malise cursed at the same time.

"Aye, ye understand now. Ye have brought the jarl's daughter to a brood of vipers," Macbeth said.

Protectors

SINCE ARRIVING AT COURT, Brodie stayed close to Orla, rarely letting her out of his sight unless she was with Queen Gruoch or in the company of his retainers.

His obsession with his wife had increased, given the dangers she faced and the fear he had of losing her. He could see the strain and stress showing on her face, and he wanted to ease some of her worries. He remained alert so she would not have to. Brodie cared nothing for his own comfort. He thought only of hers.

Macbeth had yet to receive word from Jarl Thorfinn, and until he was located and notified of Orla's existence, her life was in danger.

Dalziel also kept a close eye on Orla, and he did so not only for her sake but for Brodie's sake. It was plain to see how much Brodie loved his wife, so Dalziel used all his skills at Court to shield them both from Moddan, divulging no sensitive information.

Moddan was being elusive and rarely showed his face at gatherings.

What troubled Dalziel the most was an unshakable conviction that things were about to get worse.

Moddan

MODDAN LAY BACK IN his four-poster bed, ranting aloud, voicing his innermost secrets to his bedchamber.

"I am an earl who should be king! It grates my soul that I have spent years being an informant for Macbeth, whiling the hours away in *Caithness*. I have a campaign in *Northumbria*, building the right connections and pillaging the *Hebrides* for wealth to finance my mercenaries. All the pieces were carefully in place until Thorfinn's by-blow became an issue. Do you ken it has taken me years to drive a wedge between the earls of Orkney and the blasted jarl? And that halfwit, Rognvald, speaks to me like a child. If he had left well enough alone, everyone would have remained oblivious to her actual identity. Now, tis only a matter of time before they realize I killed Thorfinn's lover and lost my bloody hand in the process."

In frustration, Moddan focused back on the two naked maids, taking turns servicing his hard shaft with their mouths. Meanwhile, a third woman fed him her breasts to bite and suckle at will. This was the one thing he found appealing about Court life. Whores were plentiful for a man with his dark proclivities and as far as Moddan was concerned, all women were whores whether high born or lowly servant. They were there solely for his pleasure.

Feeling himself close to climaxing, he reached down and signaled to the maids to stop. With his other hand, he pointed at the woman he wanted to ride him. She immediately complied, straddling his hips and sinking down upon his rigid shaft, riding him as if her life depended on it.

When he had taken his fill, he pushed her off him and commanded the next one to ride, and then the next.

As was his habit, he decided he would spend the next few hours pounding into them in every way a man could invade a female body. While he did, he continued to share all his dirty secrets aloud. This was how he sought his release from the burdens he carried for the king.

In the morning, he would make sure his secrets died with the women.

He had lost count of the number of whores he had killed since spying for the king.

Unbeknownst to Moddan, on this occasion, there were two other people in the room, and they heard everything.

Where Angels Fear to Tread

ORLA KNEW BRODIE WAS keeping secrets from her. She had shown him the note from Malise about a person called 'Moddan' and nothing had come of it. She knew Brodie talked to Dalziel, but as yet, neither one of them divulged any information to her.

She worried about her husband since her weird conversation with Dalziel about Brodie needing protection, and she also worried about the pressure Brodie was under to keep her safe.

Brodie tried to play it off in his charming way, but she sensed his tension and frustration. It was nuanced in subtle ways, such as the way he made love to her. He took her with urgency and intensity, as if he were savoring each moment in case it was their last.

Orla knew when she married Brodie, he had a strong sexual appetite, but lately; he was insatiable. Within minutes of completion and satiation, he was ready for the next round, barely giving her time to recover before he was thrusting inside her again.

The only way to ease his anxiety was to eliminate the threat against her life.

As was her way, Orla took matters into her own hands. She needed to discover who this 'One-hand' Moddan person was and eliminate the threat once and for all.

After several discreet inquiries, with a maid and footman she had befriended, Orla found Moddan's room. The footman had assumed she was arranging a secret assignation with him and told her of a secret passageway women used that led to his chamber.

Orla slid her dagger inside her belt and slipped down the hallway when her retainers were not looking. She found the door secreted in a walled panel and slipped inside.

Moddan's room was empty. Orla searched in drawers, looking around for anything which could be of interest. She was walking around the bed when she felt a loose floorboard under the rug. Orla remembered Amelia telling her that people often hid things inside floorboards.

Orla flipped back the rug and used her dagger to pry it open.

Sure enough, there were letters wedged between the boards. She opened the first one. It was from Northumbria and referred to a *'White Bear'* and something about English ships. The rest of the letter was in French, which she could not understand. She flipped through the others, skimming the contents and recognizing the names of some places.

Orla heard footsteps nearby. She quickly pocketed the bundle and shoved the floorboard back into its place, then flipped the rug back over it. She could not leave through the main door or passageway in case they came from there.

Orla was trying to find a hiding place when someone grabbed her from behind and clamped a hand over her mouth. She stifled a scream until she heard the voice.

"Stay still!" Dalziel said as he moved them both behind an enormous set of drapes.

What was he doing here?

Dalziel hissed in her ear, "You daft woman. Brodie is going to wring your neck."

They both stilled when three women entered the room and began removing their clothing. Moments later, a large bald headed man appeared. His left hand was missing. *Moddan.*

He stripped off his clothes and joined the women on the bed. They drank some wine and began their sexual festivities.

It was not the orgy Moddan was engaging in that surprised Orla, but the secrets that spilled from his lips as he gorged himself on three women.

But when he talked of killing her mother, Orla saw red.

It took every ounce of strength Dalziel had to stop Orla from crossing the room and stabbing Moddan in the crotch.

※

AN HOUR LATER, THE four occupants lay passed out on the bed. It surprised Orla, their lack of stamina given how energetic their beginning was.

Dalziel stepped out from behind her and searched the room for something.

"Dalziel, what are you doing? They might wake up," Orla whispered.

"No, I drugged the wine. They'll be sleeping for a while. I'm just sorry it did not work faster because I will never get the sight of his hairy bollocks out of my mind!" Dalziel grimaced.

Orla just stared at Dalziel, wondering who the hell this man was.

"Are you going to kill him?" she asked.

"No, I cannot... yet. There is much at stake."

"But he killed my ma. We need to tell Macbeth."

Dalziel stopped searching, turned to Orla, and replied, "I am sorry about your ma, Orla, but I need you to trust me. I ken what to do."

Orla saw the sincerity in his eyes and nodded then asked, "What are we looking for?"

"*We* are not looking for anything. *You* are getting your person back to your husband. There's a guardsman waiting to escort you outside."

"But I can help," Orla replied as she watched Dalziel look under the furniture.

Dalziel sighed. "I'm looking for letters."

Orla reached into her pocket and pulled out the bundle. "These letters?" she asked.

Dalziel froze and stared at the parchments in her hand. "Please tell me you didn't read any of them?" he replied.

Orla averted her eyes and said, "Um..."

"Damn! No wonder Brodie was so high-strung lately. You are a menace." Dalziel grabbed Orla's arm at the elbow and dragged her out of Moddan's room.

"YOU DID WHAT?" BRODIE roared.

He was wearing a hole in the rug with the amount of pacing he had been doing since Dalziel hauled Orla into their chambers and told Brodie where he found her.

"Well, you both willna tell me anything, so I needed to find out for myself," Orla whined.

"If Moddan found you first, he would have killed you and we would not have found your body," Dalziel said.

Orla looked contrite.

Brodie just glared at her and shook his head. He turned to Dalziel and asked, "So, what happens now?"

"I will inform Macbeth."

"What do we do in the meantime?" Brodie asked.

"We give Moddan enough rope," Dalziel replied.

"For what?" Orla asked.

"To hang himself."

The Mission

THAT EVENING, DALZIEL told Macbeth everything he knew about Moddan. Leaving out Orla's involvement.

Together they went over the letters and Macbeth swore when he realized the treacherous game Moddan was playing, especially with his Northumbrian contacts.

"I hear you have an estate in Northumbria?" Macbeth asked.

"Aye, but I dinnae wish to become reacquainted with that side of my family," Dalziel replied.

"What happened? Your English mother abandoned ye?" Macbeth joked.

"Something like that. I despise all things English."

"Then you are exactly the man I need."

"What do you mean?" Dalziel asked suspiciously.

"Siward, the Stout, Earl of Northumbria, is on the move. The man is an ambitious usurper, trading on a superstitious legend that he descended from a *white bear*. His power grows daily, and he has allied with Malcolm, Duncan's son."

Dalziel knew the family history well. King Duncan mac Crìonain was Macbeth's first cousin and predecessor. Macbeth killed Duncan in battle, and now Duncan's son Malcolm III was hellbent on revenge.

"What do you want me to do?" Dalziel asked.

"I want you to take up the reins to this English estate of yours because I need you to be my eyes and ears in Northumbria."

Dalziel gritted his teeth. He would rather lie in a pit of pigs' blood. "Aye. As you wish."

"And one more thing," Macbeth said.

"What is it?"

"Once ye've settled into the estate, I need ye to marry into the gentry. A quiet, biddable English woman will do. Someone who will help you look the part of a typical nobleman without being a distraction."

"Damn it!" Dalziel cursed out loud. The last thing he wanted was to be leg shackled to a bloody upstart English female. Not to mention he had a jealous ex-mistress Lenora, who would not take kindly to news he was to marry. He had been avoiding Lenora for months. He was going to have to sort out that situation soon.

Dalziel wondered when his life had become so complicated.

His thoughts were interrupted when Macbeth said, "As for Moddan, he is now a dead man."

Trouble in Paradise

AFTER DALZIEL LEFT them, Brodie and Orla prepared for bed. It was the first night since their wedding where Brodie did not touch her. He slept on his side of the bed and with his back to her. He did not even speak to her or respond. It was like all the warmth had seeped out of their marriage.

Orla knew Brodie was angry and gave him space. She did not want to admit that she missed being tucked into his side.

Brodie was so mad at Orla's defiance and reckless behavior; he could not bring himself to even talk or touch her in case he whipped her ass raw for scaring him so much.

Instead, he put some distance between them until he could get his riotous emotions under control. He admitted he missed tucking her into his side, but he conceded it was for the best. His mind made up; Brodie drifted off to sleep.

Orla felt bereft. She could not sleep knowing her husband was angry with her. Yet her pride prevented her from doing anything about it. She made a mental note that she needed to do better to appease his worry. She would apologize to him in the morning.

That moment never came, because when she awoke, Brodie was gone. He left two retainers guarding her door, but the man himself was nowhere to be seen. It was the first time since their wedding that he did not wake her to make love or just to share breakfast together.

Orla realized how much she had become accustomed to their routines in such a short amount of time. And that worried her. *What if he never forgave her? What if he started looking elsewhere for female company?*

Orla admitted to herself for the first time she was terrified of losing Brodie. How pathetic that she was once again that vulnerable little orphan girl, desperate for the tiny scraps of attention Brodie would pay her.

Orla slapped her hand on her forehead and told herself 'No!' she would not mope around all day racked with insecurities. She needed to find something useful to occupy herself, and she knew exactly what it was.

Orla quickly washed and dressed, then headed to the archery range.

BRODIE LEFT THEIR BED-chamber early that morning. He had slept terribly, not having Orla curled into his side, but his stubborn male pride would not give in. He arose, washed, dressed, and left for the Training Grounds. He needed to spar with his men, hone their skills, or they would all grow soft around the middle like many of the male courtiers.

Sparring was also a good way to relieve the tension he had been feeling for the past fortnight.

And so it was he and his men engaged in a rigorous training session, bare-chested and glistening with perspiration, which attracted a bevy of female onlookers. Some of whom kept trying to gain his attention. There was a time he would have welcomed their advances. Not anymore. Instead, he remained focused on the task at hand.

When the men stopped for a break to quench their thirst, he heard a conversation between some male courtiers. They were commenting on how impressed they were by the skills of a woman down at the archery field. In their description, he knew they were talking about Orla. One even commented that she would make a fine mistress, but he feared her list of admirers was growing larger by the minute.

Brodie stiffened at that last comment and, without a word, he threw on his shirt and stormed across the castle grounds in search of the archery range.

Mr. Arrowsmith

ORLA LEFT HER CHAMBERS and walked through the castle grounds with retainers in tow. She had requested permission to practice at the archery range, which was a popular pastime with courtiers and ladies.

Wearing one of her new garments and slippers, she took her bow and quiver and settled in for a morning of shooting.

The range was sophisticated, with page boys on hand to assist with the retrieval of arrows and moving the targets across the field.

Soon Orla became lost in the activity. Hitting the selected targets each time.

Such was her skill and concentration Orla had not realized she had attracted an audience who clapped and cheered.

Some even came forward to challenge her, and they placed wagers.

For the first time in a long time, Orla just enjoyed herself without the threat of an attack hanging over her head.

Eventually, the noonday refreshments were served on the lawns, and Orla was inundated with male courtiers requesting archery advice. Orla was happy to oblige them.

But one man stood out from the crowd. She recognized him as the castle bowyer. He came forward carrying a beautifully handcrafted bow and quiver. It impressed Orla.

"The name's Arrowsmith. I've been wanting to make your acquaintance since you shot your first arrow."

Orla reached out her hand to shake his. "Pleased to meet you, Mr. Arrowsmith. I am Orla Fletcher."

"Your skill is impressive. May I?" He gestured towards her bow. Orla handed it over to him. He turned it over, held it to the light, and whistled. "Aye, tis a beauty this one. Yew wood, copper inlay?" he asked.

"Aye," she replied with a blush.

"Who crafted it?"

"I did," Orla replied.

He looked shocked. "And ye crafted the arrow shafts as well?"

"Aye. When I was six, my adoptive ma talked the bowyer into letting me apprentice with him."

"I bet he was none too pleased about that," Arrowsmith said.

Orla laughed. "He refused to take on a girl, but eventually he gave in and I had a talent for it, so he ceased complaining."

"I suspect he got the better end of the bargain if you produced work like this for him."

Orla stared at his bow. "Your bow is very impressive. Did you make it?"

"Aye, I sure did." He handed it to her.

Orla held it up to the light and said, "Ashwood, pearl inlay?"

"Och, I think I'm in love." He grinned. "Those are the most sensual words I've ever heard from a woman's lips."

Orla chuckled in return.

"Your bow is the most beautiful I have ever seen. You truly are a master bowyer, Mr. Arrowsmith."

He blushed bright red at her praise and in a bashful voice said, "Go on with you, tis just wood and bits of shell."

The sound of someone clearing their throat interrupted them. When Orla turned, she saw Brodie standing beside her, and he was none too pleased. Orla was so happy to see him she did not care why he was angry, only that she had missed him. Without warning, she threw her arms around his middle, stood on tiptoe, and kissed him on the cheek.

Brodie stared down at her in surprise and pulled her further into his side, smiled, and kissed her forehead.

"Mr. Arrowsmith, this is my husband, Brodie Fletcher."

"Pleased to meet you, sir, you are a vera lucky man."

"Aye, and I ken it," Brodie replied.

They shook hands before Arrowsmith excused himself.

When he left, Brodie said, "I cannot leave you for half a day without men throwing themselves at your feet."

"He was not throwing himself at my feet." Orla rolled her eyes.

"Aye, he was trying to seduce you with his pretty bow and arrows. In another ten minutes, he would have carried you off to *his bedchamber*."

Orla just grinned before she became serious. "I missed you this morning. Are you still angry with me?"

"No love, I just needed to clear my head. I was sparring with the men. But I missed you too much," Brodie replied.

"I am sorry, husband. I will not put myself in danger again. But you need to promise me that no matter how angry you are with me; you will not turn your back on me."

Brodie saw the genuine hurt in her eyes, and his heart melted. "Aye, I promise Love."

He kept gazing at her, then his demeanor suddenly changed when he said, "We need to go right now."

"Where?"

Brodie did not answer. He just picked up her bow and quiver, grabbed her hand, and marched across the lawns.

Orla hurried to keep up. She was looking around, expecting an attack at any minute. "What is it, Brodie? Is someone following us?"

"No, I was angry last night and forgot to do something important. It is now urgent."

Brodie dragged her to their chambers. He opened the doors, slammed it shut, and locked it.

"Is it something to do with Dalziel? What did you forget?" Orla asked.

Brodie dropped her weapons on the floor and started removing his clothes. "I forgot to make love to my wife, and tis unforgivable. I intend to spend the rest of the day making up for my... lapse in memory."

"Oh..." Orla gasped as Brodie stalked towards her.

SEVERAL HOURS LATER, Orla lay naked, sprawled on top of her husband. She was exhausted and gasping for air. When she finally caught her breath she said, "Brodie, remind me to make you angry more often."

Brodie burst out laughing.

Chapter 13 – The Arrival

The following week, courtiers filled the Great Hall as the noonday feast was being served. The King and Queen invited Orla and Brodie to sit at the High table as guests. The fare was rich, and the company was pleasant.

Midway through the meal, a horn started blowing in the distance, then bells started ringing. There was the sound of shuffling and running feet.

Brodie stiffened, as a weird tension descended over the hall.

Macbeth looked at Queen Gruoch and nodded. The Queen stood and hastened all the women out of the room. She grabbed Orla's arm, saying, "Come, my dear, we must go."

Orla hesitated and turned to Brodie.

Brodie squeezed her hand and said, "Go, love, I'll find you."

The guards ushered the women out. Orla turned back to see Brodie, Dalziel, and Macbeth heading towards the main doors of the Great Hall.

Orla followed the Queen through a winding labyrinth of corridors and passageways. The Queen never faltered, making turn after turn.

Some ladies screamed when one section they entered was unlit, plunging them into darkness.

"Hold your tongues lest the enemy finds us," Gruoch reprimanded.

The women became silent.

Eventually, they came to a large doorway. The guards opened it and ushered the women inside. It opened up into a grand chamber, enough to fit them with comfort. There were slits in the walls they could just see outside the castle.

"What is this room?" Orla asked.

Gruoch replied, "We are in the highest chamber above the Gatehouse. Tis the strongest part of the castle. Those slits in the wall are arrow loops. Come, I have need of your skill."

Orla followed behind the Queen, who opened another door, and inside, the room was full of weapons.

Gruoch pulled out a bow and quiver filled with double blade iron head arrows. "Here, take these and position yourself at an arrow loop. If I give the signal, fire at anyone who comes over that hill."

The other ladies in the room fretted when they realized the Queen was expecting them to fight as well and defend the castle. Some even began weeping.

Gruoch scowled. "Ladies! Cease the hysterics. If you cannot fire a weapon, then move away from the walls."

All except two women moved away from the walls.

Queen Gruoch shook her head in disgust and muttered, "No wonder we lost the *Battle of Brunanburh*!"

They waited and stood at the ready. Orla kept her eyes on the horizon.

After what seemed like forever, a rider came forward waving a banner.

"Hold," Queen Gruoch said.

When he came closer, the banner was more prominent. It was a serpent against a white mark.

A row of Norsemen waited along the hillside, just out of range of the archers' longbows.

It surprised Orla when Gruoch cursed and dropped her bow. "That bloody idiot! Trust him to arrive with no warning."

"Whose banner is that?" a woman asked.

Gruoch replied, "Tis the banner of Norway, and that big lout in the middle of those riders is Macbeth's cousin, Jarl Thorfinn of Orkney."

Orla stilled and gazed over the horizon. No one else in the room realized what she did. She was staring at her father.

JARL THORFINN AND KING Magnus and their men rode through the main gates of Macbeth's fortified castle. The portcullis was raised, and they gathered in the inner bailey.

Macbeth boomed in an irritated voice, "Why did you not send a missive? We thought you were invaders. My men could have killed you!"

"Ha, they can try," Thorfinn replied. "I wanted to test your defences."

Macbeth asked, "Thorfinn, please tell me you didn't attack any of my men?"

"Hmm, just a handful. They will be fine once they sleep it off. Ye need to keep them on their toes. Kill a few to motivate the others."

Macbeth just shook his head. King Magnus sat on his horse beside Thorfinn and found the interaction between the cousins humorous.

Thorfinn made the formal introductions, and King Macbeth greeted King Magnus with the reverence and respect he deserved. Magnus decided he liked this king of Alba, and he was glad he insisted on traveling with Thorfinn.

Once they greeted the courtiers and other members of the royal family, they were shown to special chambers reserved only for visiting dignitaries. It gave them time to rest before they attended the welcome feast.

The castle was in a frenzy with a Jarl of Orkney and the King of Norway visiting at the same time. The only person not jubilant was Moddan. Not only had someone drugged him and stolen his secret letters, but he had also awoken to an empty bed with no trace of the maids. To make matters worse the Jarl of Orkney was in the same castle as his long lost daughter. Moddan could see all his carefully laid plans unraveling. He was becoming desperate, and a desperate man was a dangerous one.

THAT NIGHT ORLA, BRODIE, and Dalziel sat talking in the sitting room of their guest bed chambers. Macbeth thought it wise that Orla remain out of sight until he could arrange a private meeting with Thorfinn.

Orla was too nervous to go back to the Great Hall for festivities, so she was happy with the plan. Brodie was also fine with it because he wanted to keep Orla close now that there were more people in the Keep.

They needed to prepare themselves for the meeting. It was a good thing they took the time to rest because the next day their lives were going to change irrevocably.

The Tempest

THE FOLLOWING DAY, the Queen organized a private luncheon in the Upper Hall, allowing the King to entertain their distinguished guests in private. Brodie, Orla, Torstein, and Dalziel were also in attendance with a small retinue. The guests milled about the room, taking refreshments as they waited for Jarl Thorfinn and King Magnus.

A hush came over the group as Jarl Thorfinn Sigurdsson entered the hall.

His aura siphoned all the air from the room. He cut a menacing figure with shoulder-length black hair and bushy eyebrows. His face held a frightful severity. Defined cheekbones, broad nose, stern lips, and shrewd eyes. He wore trews, boots, and a fur-lined vest over a long-sleeved tunic. His fingers were adorned with large silver rings. Ink markings lined his neck and hands. He looked every bit a Viking.

There was nothing friendly about him.

Orla shuddered at the sight of him. There was no warmth at all. He radiated violence, and she wondered if there was any softness to such a man.

King Magnus was ushered to the dais, where he took a seat beside Queen Gruoch, and Jarl Thorfinn stood beside Macbeth.

Thorfinn spoke in gruff tones to Macbeth, who seemed unruffled. "Whit is dis? Why was I summoned from my rest?" He paced, agitated. There was no peace, as if his mind constantly ticked.

"Calm, cousin. I have invited you here among friends because I wish to introduce you to someone special," Macbeth replied.

"Vera, well, get it over with. I've no patience for formalities," Thorfinn grumbled.

Thorfinn looked about the room when he caught sight of Orla. He stopped dead in his tracks and just stared. His fierce gaze pinning her to the spot.

Orla stilled. A myriad of emotions crossed Thorfinn's features she could not keep up. He was looking directly at her and only at her.

"Izara?" he said as a strangled cry left Thorfinn's lips. He leaped from the dais and stormed towards her. His features contorted to reflect the discomfiture of a raging tempest within.

Orla was trembling. Jarl Thorfinn grabbed her by the arms, and he started shaking her. "Who are you? Whit is dis?" he roared.

Too shocked to react, Orla felt the jarring effect of his actions. His turmoil was palpable. And Orla witnessed something cross his expression. *Agony.* In his eyes, she saw it then. It was pain, soul-deep, unfathomable pain.

She heard Macbeth and the Queen both shouting, "Thorfinn, cease!"

Then Brodie shouted, "Dinnae touch her!"

Orla lost sight of Jarl Thorfinn. The hands that clutched her arms released, and instead, she was pushed backward. The jarl disappeared and all she saw was Brodie's back, directly in front of her. His hand resting on the pommel of his sword, ready to battle. Ever the protector, Brodie stood between her and an unyielding force.

"You dare defy me?" Thorfinn bellowed.

"Aye, I protect what is mine!" Brodie roared in return.

Orla did not want Brodie thrown in the dungeon. He was in the King's castle. He could not attack a nobleman.

"Brodie…" she said, placing a hand on his shoulder. "Please dinnae make any trouble with the jarl."

She peeked out from behind Brodie. Her eyes met Thorfinn's again. "I beg your forgiveness, Jarl Thorfinn."

Orla furrowed her brow, trying to read Thorfinn's mood.

Thorfinn noted her expression, and a change came over him. His eyes softened immediately, then he smiled as his entire demeanor gentled.

Given the severity of his facial features, his smile was scarier than his scowl, but Orla willed herself not to flinch.

Macbeth approached them. "Cousin! Is this any way to treat my guests?" He raised his eyebrow, then said to Brodie, "Ye can stand down now. I believe there is much we need to discuss."

Family Reunion

IN THE PRIVACY OF A small chamber next to the Upper Hall, Thorfinn 'the Mighty' Jarl of Orkney formally met his long-lost daughter. He also clenched his fists as he sat through the explanation of how she came to be at Macbeth's castle. He made a mental note that anyone involved in the death of his beloved Izara would die a gruesome death.

Long gone was the gruff, menacing man who initially greeted Orla in the hall. A softer, kinder version replaced him. One who insisted she sit beside him and ordered servants about, ensuring she had enough to eat and drink. He even had a maid bring a fur-lined cloak for her to wear because the room felt chilly.

Brodie was pleased Orla had time to speak with her sire, but he was in a dark mood because he could not get near her. Such was the level of fuss Thorfinn made over her. And only towards her. To everyone else, the jarl behaved like a disagreeable tyrant.

Brodie bided his time as he stood patiently beside Dalziel, watching Orla bask in the glory of her father's attention. But what disturbed him the most was the rapt attention King Magnus seemed to pay his wife.

Magnus gazed at Orla like she was an oasis in a desert and he was parched. Brodie knew that look because that was how he viewed his wife. He clenched his jaw when Magnus offered to hand feed Orla some grapes. Orla politely declined, which was a good thing, or Brodie would have ended up in the dungeons for murdering a reigning monarch.

Dalziel quietly observed everyone in the room. He did not miss Magnus's interest in Orla or the affection Thorfinn had for his newfound daughter.

He had a gut feeling it was going to become an issue. Dalziel just hoped the contingency plans he had in place were enough to safeguard Brodie and Orla.

THORFINN WAS STILL reeling from the knowledge that he had a daughter. His mind was already strategizing his next moves. Uppermost was giving her everything she had missed out on in life. He wanted the world to know who she was, and that she was now under his protection.

Thorfinn said, "You look so much like your *mor*. Right down to the confused furrow of your brow. Izara always gave me that look when she was unsure."

"Was she happy?" Orla asked.

"Aye, it did not start out that way. I had captured her on a raid and by the gods did she fight me like a valkyrie. But I never touched her with violence. I loved her with my very being."

"Did she love you in return?" Orla needed to know what her mother experienced.

"Aye, eventually she softened towards me. We eagerly awaited your birth. I even offered to let her visit her homeland once you were safely delivered."

"Where were you when she passed?" Orla asked.

"Raiding Scotland?" Macbeth asked with a questioning brow.

"No, I was in Norway discussing the control of Orkney with King Olaf."

"Would you have really let her visit her homeland?" Magnus asked.

"Aye. But she never got around to telling me who her family was."

Orla noticed a look of concern cross Macbeth's face before he masked it.

"So, what is your full name?" Thorfinn asked.

"My name is Orla, but I did not have a last name until—"

Thorfinn cut her off. "Your name should be Zala, it wis Izara's choice if she had a girl and your last name is Thorfinnsdottir."

"No, her last name is Fletcher!" Brodie growled.

"Who is this irritating man?" Thorfinn rumbled in exasperation. He looked at Macbeth and tilted his head towards Brodie. "Well, Macbeth? Are you gan to remove him, or shall I?"

"Jarl Thorfinn, there is no need. He is my husband, Brodie Fletcher of the MacGregor clan."

"You will call me *Far* from now on... and you... married that man?" Thorfinn pointed at Brodie.

"Aye, I love him."

Brodie smiled at his wife's declaration.

Thorfinn frowned and rose from his chair. "Macbeth, I *mis* speak to you." He rumbled.

They moved away from the others.

"I want that marriage annulled. As her *far* I should be the one to choose her husband and I dinnae like the one she has. He's... defiant," Thorfinn said.

"Cousin, the marriage is legal and attested to by the church, and they have consummated it."

"The marriage wis illegal because *I* did not consent."

"Come now, Thorfinn, she is happy. There is no political gain in nullifying her marriage."

"I want my *dattar* to come back with me to Orkney and marry a nobleman. I dinnae want that man with her. His eyes are shifty," Thorfinn grumbled.

Macbeth sighed. "That man has protected her all his life. The only reason ye dinnae like him is because he is not afraid of ye."

"Aye, precisely. Tis proof he is touched in the head." Thorfinn scowled.

"Your *nighean* willna let him go, so ye best put that idea away if ye want a good relationship with her."

Thorfinn just scowled. "We shall see."

When they returned to the others, it surprised them to witness King Magnus making open advances towards Orla.

Thralls and Concubines

ORLA SAT BESIDE THE king of Norway, feeling a little uncomfortable. She wanted to go to Brodie, but King Magnus kept talking. They called him 'Magnus the Good' as he was a man of high morals and principles.

Although only nineteen summers, he seemed older than his age. He was nothing like she would have imagined for a boy-king. There was nothing boyish about his physique. He was tall and muscular. No stranger to hard work and battle, as his calloused hands attested.

But it was his manner that impressed Orla. There was kindness in his eyes when he smiled and when he spoke, he was articulate and confident and assured in his stride.

Orla noticed King Magnus stared a great deal at her. He had even reached out and swept an errant curl away from her face.

"Did you know your *mor* was to be a gift to my far, King Olaf?" Magnus asked.

Orla just shook her head, surprised by the revelation.

"Tis true, but the jarl kept her for himself. It must have been genuine love if he defied a King over it."

"Was King Olaf displeased?" Orla asked.

Magnus chuckled. "Not at all. Besides, my *far* already had an English concubine... my mother Alfhild who now lives in my palace in Norway. She was Queen Astrid's lady-in-waiting and become my *far's* concubine."

"Was there a scandal? Given that she was close to Queen Astrid?"

Magnus grinned. "The biggest scandal in history. No one knew until my *mor* started showing and King Olaf confessed the child was his. Queen Astrid also lives in my palace. She and my *mor*... let's just say they dislike one another with passion."

"How do you keep the peace?" Orla asked.

"I make sure they are never in the same room at the same time. If they are, I have guards standing between them because once, at a banquet, Astrid tore out my *mor's* wig."

Orla opened her mouth in disbelief and said, "No..."

"It's true. The wig landed on the head of the roast boar."

Orla and Magnus shared a look, then both started giggling like children. When they composed themselves after Brodie cleared his throat loudly several times, Magnus said, "It's ironic no, that the daughter of a thrall and a son of a concubine would be here now, together, feasting at the table of kings."

"Aye, you are insightful for one so young."

"Maybe it is fate that has brought us together?" He raised an eyebrow.

Was the king of Norway flirting with her? Orla was uncertain. She heard a small growl coming from Brodie and when she looked over at him; he was clenching his fists but did not move from Dalziel's side.

"I was eleven when I came to the throne. Did you know that?" Magnus asked.

"It must have been difficult for one so young." Orla empathized.

"And this year I also became king of Denmark. It is a significant change for a child, who came into the world, struggling for his first breath."

"'Tis truly a remarkable feat Your Majesty."

Magnus seemed contemplative. "I was born early and not expected to survive the night because I could barely breathe. But God had other plans. Not only did I keep breathing, but I grew stronger each day. I learned to conquer and not be conquered, and I surrounded myself with excellent advisors." He paused, then reached out and brushed the back of his hand across Orla's cheek.

"So, you see. I am very blessed and have much to offer the right woman."

"It sounds like destiny, Your Majesty."

"Please call me Magnus. We are closer in age and I feel ancient when you refer to me in such formal tones. I would love to hear my name fall from your lips with ease." He gave her a poignant look. "You are exquisite, Orla," he whispered as he moved his chair closer. "Mayhap you would consider coming with me when I return to Norway?"

Orla could feel the tension coming from Brodie. She blushed then said, "I am flattered, Your Maj—"

"Magnus, call me Magnus," he interrupted.

"Uh... Magnus."

Magnus closed his eyes when Orla said his name, then opened them and said, "Please say my name again."

"Magnus?"

Magnus smiled at her then. "It is as if an angel from the heavens spoke my name."

Brodie snorted out loud, and Dalziel tried hard to not laugh. Orla was feeling uncomfortable.

"You were saying?" Magnus asked.

"Oh, ah yes, Magnus, I am flattered, but I cannot leave Scotland. My life is here with my husband."

"Aye!" Brodie shouted from the other side of the table before Dalziel kicked him in the shin.

Magnus ignored Brodie and just stared at Orla before sighing. "Well, it is a pity, my rare beauty. We will revisit this talk again soon."

By then, Macbeth and Thorfinn had returned to the table, and Magnus pulled away from Orla.

On Edge

THAT NIGHT, WHEN THEY returned to their bedchamber, Brodie was on edge.

It had been hours since he had touched Orla because the reunion went on forever. The torture of being denied access to his own wife had him feeling like a caged animal.

His possessive tendencies had escalated since Magnus started openly flirting with her, and Brodie viscerally needed to claim his woman all over again.

Which he did several times all over their bedroom chamber. He took her in front of the fireplace, inside their shared bath, on the table, on the on the window nook, against the door. Any flat surface he could take her, he did until he could calm down again.

Orla did not complain, although she was currently passed out beside him on the bed.

Brodie lay on his back and held her tight as he stared at the ceiling.

He was certain the threat to her life was over now that Thorfinn knew of her existence and they could return to Glenorchy.

Brodie would soon find out how wrong he was.

Chapter 14 – Family Ties

Royal Palace, Lake Hayq, Abyssinia

Zenabu, Queen Gudit's advisor for many years, had never put a foot wrong. He was a loyal subject, and he would serve his beloved queen until he died.

Over the years, he had gained much power and privilege, and it had been his greatest accomplishment organizing the retrieval of Prince Kato from the clutches of a madman.

But all would come to nothing if something happened to the prince.

Zenabu had woken with a bad feeling that something was amiss. He immediately went in search of Kato and hoped the prince was not getting himself into mischief. Kato had a strong will and innate ability to attract trouble. The prince was a skilled warrior and a good fighter, but he always pushed the boundaries.

Zenabu knew it was because Kato was born to lead and someday, he would make a powerful king. But a ruler was only effective if they knew when to act, and when to be still and listen. Zenabu had a bad feeling that Kato was about to push the boundaries too far.

He had just entered the family's private solar when he heard Queen Gudit shouting.

Despite his age, Zenabu could still run, and he did so. When he burst into the Queen's study, he saw her hunched over a letter and cursing.

"What is it, my *Nigisiti*?"

"Kato. That foolhardy grandson of mine..."
"What has the *Li'uli* done now?"
"He has gone to Scotland!"

Kinrossie, Perthshire, Scotland

AJANI NURU, *'The Seeker'* of *Habesha*, had traveled many miles searching for a woman he failed to rescue when she was a baby. It was a regret he held for many years. At the time, he had mere moments to save two babes, but the hand fate dealt him meant he could only spare one. He chose and abandoned one child to save another.

Now he could redeem himself and complete his promise to his queen.

Through his intricate web of scouts and informants, he had contacted the king of Scotland and was close to claiming his prize.

Ajani camped in woodlands near the castle fort, studying the movements of the people within, learning their weak points.

Men like Ajani were born *seekers*. They could find anything and anyone. They lived quietly in the shadows, making their presence known only when they deemed the time was right.

He had already been inside Macbeth's castle several times, always in a different disguise to hide his skin. He had even followed the king for a day perched high above the rafters. It amazed him how rarely people looked up.

In his wanderings about the castle walls, Ajani had discovered one thing.

No matter their race, creed, or color, the hearts of men were often treacherous.

Ajani knew what dangers awaited the princess.

As he sharpened the sickle curved blades of his shotel swords, he vowed that this time, he would not abandon her to the unknown.

Ajani heard a leaf rustle behind him. He twirled around, ready to strike with his blade, then stared in astonishment. "*Li'uli* Kato, what are you doing here?"

⁂

Rose Garden, Macbeth's Castle

A DAY AFTER THEIR FIRST meeting, Thorfinn had requested Orla join him for a walk in Queen Gruoch's rose gardens.

Thorfinn wanted private time away from everyone to get to know his daughter better.

As they meandered through the gardens, he said, "Your mother was exquisite. She was also adept at using weapons. When she fought with swords, it was like a valkyrie riding into battle."

Orla thought about the dream she had of her mother. "How was she with swords?"

"Izara always fought with two swords, one in each hand. She would twirl them with her wrists and shift her body weight from side to side."—Thorfinn showed the movements by lifting his arms out to his side and twirling his wrists using imaginary swords. He then shifted his weight from one foot to the other, pivoting back and forth. "She could always anticipate my next move."

"You used to train with her?"

Thorfinn resumed walking and said, "Aye, I loved it. It was exhilarating. Her skills were exceptional. She had the blacksmith fashion, a particular sword she called a 'shotel'. They curved the blade like a semicircle. It was effective because the blade could curve around a man's shield and hook them in the side."

"Do you still have this sword?"

"No, after the fire, I could not find any trace of it."

"What was she like?"

Thorfinn was silent for a moment, then replied, "She was my peace. She calmed the raging tempest within me with the quiet strength and formidable resilience. It was as if she was born to be a queen."

"Do you regret capturing her?"

"Sometimes, but if I had not done it, I would never have kenned that kind of love could exist between two people. I am but a selfish man." He shrugged his shoulders.

They walked in silence as Orla contemplated what he said.

"Are you married now? Is there a wife in the Orkneys?"

Thorfinn sighed. "Not yet, but there will be soon. I mourned a long time after Izara passed. But I have since found a good, gentle woman who has helped me heal. She reminds me a lot of Izara."

"I am glad that you have found her. What is her name?"

"Ingibiorg Finnsdottir, a gentlewoman. I am determined to make her happy."

"Why do you frown?" Orla asked.

"I always feel like an ugly ogre next to gentlewomen."

"*Far*, you are not an ugly ogre to me."

"Then I fear you may have a sight impediment, *dattar*."

Orla burst out laughing.

He smiled and said, "You remind me of your *mor* when you laugh."

They spent the next two hours sharing about their lives and talking of weapons and the latest in Viking ships. Orla even agreed to fashion a bow for Thorfinn while he arranged a sword to be made for her bearing the Orkney crest.

By the end of their time together, Thorfinn had decided that Orla was too good for a meager Scottish clan. He wanted her wielding her own power and gracing the halls of a royal court. He would see it done.

BRODIE REMAINED CLOSE by, but a pit formed in his stomach. Orla was not an orphan but, in fact, the daughter of a powerful jarl, the great-granddaughter of a past Scottish king and a cousin to the current king. She really was too good for him, although she always had been. Brodie felt beneath her. There was still no way he was giving her up. He believed deep in his soul that they were destined to be together.

The King's Study

"MODDAN IS IN THE WIND," Macbeth said to Dalziel.

"How?"

"He killed two of the men I sent to follow him. He was to meet me and Thorfinn last night for a private meeting but didn't show."

"I will send out a hunt," Dalziel said.

"Malise is also searching for him in case he has headed to the Hebrides."

"What about Orla? Is it safe for her to return to Glenorchy now that Thorfinn kens of her existence?" Dalziel asked.

"About that… tis a wee bit more complicated now," Macbeth replied.

"How so?"

"Take a seat Dalziel, I need your keen mind to work a way out of this mess."

Dalziel braced himself. He knew he was about to receive information he would not like.

The Great Hall

DURING THE AFTERNOON'S repast, Brodie and Orla sat together in the Great Hall. They were seated at a special trestle table just below the dais when Dalziel joined them.

"We have a problem," he whispered.

"What is it?" Brodie asked.

"Thorfinn wants your marriage annulled."

"What?" Brodie clenched his fists.

"He cannot do that?" Orla hissed.

"Aye, he can. He has requested Macbeth petition Rome for a formal annulment, citing his lack of consent as your da."

Brodie and Orla looked shocked.

"Over my dead body! She is my wife even now she could be carrying my bairn," Brodie hissed.

"But why? What does he expect to gain out of this?" Orla was livid, to think after a lovely time spent in the gardens, her father could demand an annulment.

"King Magnus wants Orla in Norway with him, and he has offered to grant Thorfinn a bigger share of Orkney in return," Dalziel replied.

Brodie pulled Orla closer to his side. "King Magnus can go to the devil! This is my wife and I willna let him take her."

"Tis politics and power play, Brodie. Your marriage has become a complicated matter. But calm yourselves. I merely came to warn you lest you hear from another source. I need you to trust me."

"Aye, thank you, Brother," Brodie said in a defeated voice.

"I cannot believe he would do this to me?" Orla said. All her life Orla wished she had kin, but now she wished she were plain Orla the Orphan again.

Chapter 15 – Wooden Doors

The Smithy

Macbeth's Castle was a fortified monolith created to keep any threat out. What they had not expected was the threat from within the castle itself.

The surprise attack came swiftly. No one was ready for it, least of all the king.

The morning had started the same as all previous mornings. Brodie made love to his wife. They bathed and broke their fast together, then he was called away to see to his men.

Orla tried to talk to her father about the annulment. However, Thorfinn was actively avoiding her, and King Magnus was suspiciously unavailable.

Angry and frustrated, she headed to the Smithy where they kept raw materials for weapons and armor. She intended to fashion a bow for Queen Gruoch, who asked about Orla's designs.

The guards let her in through the gated doors near the Forge, and she was given free rein to work in the guild apprentices section.

While Orla was rummaging through a back chamber gathering raw materials, she felt a weird tension in the air. From her vantage point, she was hidden behind piles of materials, which enabled her to observe people openly. Some were nervous, and one apprentice kept glancing at the postern gate.

Orla saw the gate open from the outside, which was unusual, as it should be locked. Then she saw men pouring in. She heard her name being mentioned and others pointed towards the back chamber. Her heart started pounding faster. They were looking for her.

It startled Orla when someone tapped her on the shoulder.

She spun around to see Arrowsmith, the bowyer. He was holding his bow in one hand and two arrows in the other. He was staring at her, his eyes kept signaling to her right.

The only thing to her right was a wooden door. Orla reached out to touch it and Arrowsmith nodded and mouthed a silent, "Go."

Her instinct told her to run. Orla opened the door and before it closed behind her, she turned back to see Arrowsmith pull up his bow, simultaneously nock two arrows, and aim at the postern gate.

Orla plunged down a dimly lit passageway and ran. She could hear shouts coming from the outer wall and thanked the heavens Arrowsmith had found her when he did because the castle was under siege.

Siege

BRODIE AND HIS MEN were at the training grounds when he heard the bells ringing. The castle was under siege. His driving instinct was to head to the Great Hall. It was the place he and Orla had agreed to meet if they were ever separated within the castle.

But the enemy had already infiltrated the bailey. The MacGregor warriors instantly went into battle mode, grabbing swords, shields, and battle-axes. They stood in formation, then Brodie shouted the war cry and, as one cohesive unit, they moved. Cutting down mercenaries in their path.

Brodie saw flashes of black hair and golden hair fighting alongside him and turned to see Thorfinn and his men join the battle. Norsemen and Scotsmen fought as one. Both sides protecting the reigning monarchs. Together, their fighting abilities overpowered the disorganized mercenaries as they moved as one army inside the castle.

Brodie sprinted towards the Great Hall, battle axe in one hand and sword in the other, dispatching any enemy who came across his path. His one thought was to get to his wife.

Melee

ORLA STUMBLED AROUND in the narrow passageways for what felt like forever. She could not find a way out. She cursed castles with a labyrinth of inner walls. *Who designed these things? It could only be a man!*

Orla worried about Brodie, Arrowsmith, the MacGregor retainers, Thorfinn and the King and Queen, and all the servants inside the walls. She was working herself up into hysterical panic and she knew it, but dark confined spaces with no doors had never been her strong suit.

Breath and stay calm. She kept repeating to herself as she ran, looking for an opening or doorway in the walls.

Finally, Orla hit a hollow wooden panel. She pushed it open with such force she fell face-first into a long, empty corridor. She rolled, stood, and moved against the wall as she tried to get her bearings to the Great Hall.

She needed to head up. Orla found a staircase. It looked clear; she sprinted up the stairs and made it to the first landing. Orla sprinted across a hallway of chamber doors, and when she rounded the corner, it looked familiar. She was close and knew where the secret passageway was that could lead her to the back of the Great Hall.

Ten minutes later, Orla was in the back chamber of the hall. It relieved her to find it empty, but it did not stay that way for long. No sooner had she entered it than two men burst through the other door a few meters away. One said, "That's her!"

Orla did not hesitate. She reached back and pulled her bow out with her left hand and grabbed two arrows with her right. In quick succession, she nocked, aimed, and fired one arrow after another. Her aim struck true, and both men lay bleeding out on the carpet.

Orla pulled the arrows out of their chests, then ran into the hall. She stood with her back against the wall, staring from the dais, scanning the room for Brodie.

Men engaged in combat across the hall. She picked off mercenaries one by one with her bow and arrows. Hoping Brodie would arrive soon.

She had absolute faith that he would find her, but she had run out of arrows and more men were filing into the hall. Orla flung her bow over her shoulder and pulled out her knives. It would come down to hand-to-hand combat.

It was then she felt a prickly feeling. The hairs on the back of her neck stood on end. She looked across the dais and made eye contact with pure evil. Moddan.

He had a salacious grin. He held his sword and pointed it at her, then charged.

Orla braced and did exactly as Dalziel taught her. She slowed her breathing, focused on the blades in her hands as if they were extensions of her body, and she waited for Moddan, observing his every move. When he was close, she dropped to the floor at the last minute and slashed her dirk across the back of his legs. She heard him cry in pain and stumble sideways. Orla then rolled and stood behind him and slashed the back of his thigh. Moddan regained his balance and turned around.

He looked shocked. "You fucking whore!" he shouted, then ran at her again, this time swinging his sword.

Orla moved backward, barely dodging his blade. She stumbled and fell off the dais, landing right in the melee of fighting men.

Orla rolled out of the way of battling swords and belly crawled across the floor slashing her blades and weaving her way through a sea of mercenaries. All the while, Moddan kept stalking her.

Eventually, Orla gained her footing and made it to a wall but was trapped, between hostile men and Moddan.

She wondered where the hell Brodie was. She hoped she lived long enough to slap his face for choosing the Great Hall as their meeting point. *The worst plan ever!*

Chapter 16 – Two Worlds Collide

Mercenaries came pouring through the doors of the Great Hall, hell-bent on taking the throne and killing Orla.

Brodie arrived at the hall and his heart lodged in his throat when he saw Orla fall off the dais.

He roared and ran straight into the crowd of fighters, cutting and slashing a path desperately trying to reach her.

He saw her find her feet, and for a moment he felt relief until he spotted a man trying to attack her left side. Brodie took his battle axe and hurled it through the air, it lodged in the attacker's forehead.

Brodie saw Moddan gaining on her, and he fought harder to get to her with his sword and fist. Brodie sliced and cut mercenaries as he pushed forward, not even feeling the bloody cuts and slices against his own body. He was surviving on pure adrenalin alone.

But no matter how hard he tried, he could not reach Orla.

Moddan was moving towards Orla now, cutting down the last man who stood in his way, leaving the way open to get to her. He was a few feet away, his sword poised, aiming straight for Orla's heart.

Brodie knew Orla was about five seconds away from death, and that sense of helplessness and the inevitability of death assailed him. He knew nothing he did would stop this madman. Moddan had killed Izara and now he would kill Orla, and all the men who protected her would fail again.

"No!" The guttural roar that left Brodie's throat was visceral. He was going to watch his beloved get slaughtered before his eyes.

Desperation, panic, love, and failure warred as one within him as he desperately tried to push forward.

Dalziel entered the room so did Thorfinn, all of them trying to reach Orla. But men blocked their path.

Orla braced herself against the wall, watching her life flash before her eyes, her only regret that she had not said one last goodbye to the man she loved the most on earth. She staggered sideways. The crowd parted and Moddan stood before her, murder in his eyes. There was no way Orla could prevent Moddan's blade from cutting her. He stepped forward, a wicked smirk on his face as he brought his sword crashing down.

This was it. Orla took a deep breath and braced, ready to meet her maker when as if in slow motion, something dropped from above. Not something, *someone*. A flash of movement, a flicker of a long robe, the sound of material flapping in the breeze, before a dark-skinned warrior with a keening cry landed sure-footed directly in front of Orla. He held two curved swords with long blades in each hand, *shotels*. The likes she had never seen. He lashed the hooked end forward like a whip, and it stabbed Moddan in his side. While his other blade hooked around Moddan's sword and flung it out of Moddan's hand.

Moddan shouted in pain as the sword's curved end dug into his flesh. He clutched his side.

The warrior then twirled the swords with his wrists and swiveled left-to-right with his feet. He crossed the blades in front of him, then flicked them out to his sides. He paused a moment as he held his blades suspended in the air, taking the measure of the men surrounding him, and then he unleashed unholy hell on the unsuspecting mercenaries.

Orla stared in wonder as the warrior single-handedly cut down five men in quick succession. They had no chance against the rotating blades. They cut even men with shields because the swords curved around and pierced their backs.

Moddan had already backed away, using men as cover against the vicious, fast-moving blades. Panic was written on his face as men screamed in horror around him, never having encountered a foe or weapon such as this.

Then a second warrior dropped from above wearing similar robes, and he flanked Orla's other side, cutting down more men who dared approach. Orla felt an instant bond with him. Their skin tone was the same, their eyes were the same, their hair the same. As if an innate understanding passed between them, soul-deep. Orla knew she was staring at her twin.

The warriors then stood in front of Orla as the tide turned within the hall and the mercenaries fled. No one dared approach the two strangers for fear of being hooked by their long blades.

Brodie breathed a sigh of relief as he got closer. The two men turned towards him before Orla yelled, "No, he belongs to me!"

Brodie moved straight to Orla and swept her into his arms. She wept when she saw him, then slapped his face for choosing the Great Hall as a meeting place. The others just watched with amusement.

They heard trumpets outside the castle, a sign that the insurgence was over, and the enemy was scattering and running for the hills.

By this time, Orla had composed herself. She noticed Dalziel stood over Moddan. He was still alive but in terrible shape, losing a lot of blood.

Thorfinn came across to her and froze when he saw the young man barring his way.

"Who are you?" Thorfinn asked with a frown.

"Who is asking?" Kato replied with a scowl.

At that moment, they looked so alike. Their mannerisms even their size, and the way they both tilted their heads to size one another up. Neither backing down.

"I believe this is my twin brother and your son," Orla said.

Thorfinn inhaled sharply and whispered, "Son?"

Kato was at a loss for words. He looked at Ajani, who confirmed, "This is your sire."

Kato then turned to Thorfinn and growled, "Where the hell were you? We had to do all the work!"

Thorfinn looked shocked.

Brodie stifled a laugh.

"*Li'uli!*" Ajani reprimanded him. "Do not speak to elders that way."

Brodie addressed Ajani. "I am grateful for your help. You saved my wife's life, and I will be forever in your debt."

Ajani responded, "There is no debt. I would do anything for the princess."

He moved towards Orla, placed one hand over his heart, and bowed. "*Li'iliti*; I am Ajani, your humble servant. I have searched many years for you. I am happy to serve you."

Orla just launched herself at Ajani and hugged him. "Thank you," she said.

Ajani looked embarrassed and said, "Please Princess, it is my job to serve."

The others looked confused. So did Orla. "I am not a princess."

"Yes, you are. You are the daughter of Princess Izara, the granddaughter of Queen Gudit of Abyssinia, and you are my sister," Kato replied.

Orla just stood, stunned. "I dinnae ken what any of that means."

"I think tis time we all talked," Macbeth said. He was now standing on the dais with his guardsman surrounded by carnage.

"Aye, it seems there is much to discuss," Thorfinn grumbled.

A Mother's Love

SEVERAL HOURS LATER, after the castle was put to right, Macbeth called a meeting of Orla's family in the Upper Hall. It was here all parties formally introduced themselves and discussed their role in this complicated family saga.

Macbeth and Ajani had already spoken a sennight earlier. They had agreed on a private meeting so Orla could meet her kinsmen when the siege happened.

Queen Gudit's message to her granddaughter was straight forward. If Orla was unhappy living in Scotland, Ajani would return her to Abyssinia, where she would take her rightful place as a member of the royal family.

Thorfinn and Kato spent some time talking, and it seemed Kato was warming to his sire, although he was still angry because Thorfinn kidnapped his mother and caused much grief to his grandmother.

Orla spent time with Ajani learning everything she could about her mother's homeland and still in disbelief that her mother was a princess and her twin brother had survived.

It was over a meal that Ajani told the story of Orla's origins to everyone in the room.

Ajani explained that Orla's grandmother ruled a kingdom stretching from *Abyssinia* to *Yemnat,* a vast region. *Zeila* was a trading port where Viking raiders had traversed. The day Izara disappeared, she had slipped past her guards to explore alone.

"Like *mother*, like daughter," Brodie muttered to himself.

Ajani had tracked Izara to Orkney, but by the time he found her, the stronghold was on fire. Someone had locked Izara and her babies inside a room. A lady's maid, Runa, was trying to get the door open. When Ajani knocked the door down, Izara was already dying from a knife wound to her chest, but she had sheltered her children.

"Princess Izara asked me and Runa to protect you both. We promised we would," Ajani said. "But I could not travel with two babies without arousing suspicion, and I only had a small window of time to return to Abyssinia."

Ajani looked at Orla and said, "I am sorry, I had to leave you behind. If I left Kato, the danger would be greater for him as a male heir. Runa agreed it would be easier for her to hide a girl. That day, I left with Kato and Runa took you with her."

Orla said, "Dinnae trouble yourself. I understand now."

Ajani continued, "I intended to return for you, but war besieged my country and travel was impossible for a few years. When I was free to travel, I could not find Runa or you. We had given up hope until word reached me that there was a rumor of a mixed-race Viking woman living among the Scots."

"Do ye ken who killed Izara?" Thorfinn asked. He was still seething at the details of Izara's death. He hated himself even more for not protecting her.

"Your half-brothers sent the men that killed Izara," Ajani replied.

Thorfinn and Macbeth exchanged a knowing look. Thorfinn's eyes blazed with fury and Orla suspected if Moddan was still alive in the dungeons, he would not survive the night.

LATER THAT NIGHT, BRODIE and Orla were in bed discussing the day's events.

Brodie said, "You have more royal blood in you than anyone on earth. If you want to return to your real home—."

"My home is with you, Brodie Fletcher. You are my prince, and you are my home," Orla replied.

He kissed her lips.

Bounty

LATE THAT NIGHT, A missive arrived from Beiste MacGregor informing Dalziel that the clan had become inundated with constant attacks from raiders searching for Orla. Beiste said someone had placed a large bounty on her life, attracting mercenaries and invaders of all kinds. Jarl Thorfinn needed to acknowledge Orla was under his protection.

Torture Chamber

"YE KILLED MY WOMAN and tried to kill my children. Do you have any last words?" Thorfinn asked Moddan.

"Aye, I dinnae regret it. Your woman cut off my hand and killed two of my brothers. I curse the day I ever laid eyes on a blasted earl of Orkney!"

Thorfinn dug the tip of his golden spear deeper into Moddan's side. Moddan screamed in pain.

"You will tell me who else threatens my *dattar's* life," Thorfinn demanded.

"What do I care? Ye'll kill me, anyway." Moddan spat blood on the ground.

Thorfinn replied, "I kenned you would say that, which is why my men are preparing to travel to a house in *Caithness* where a woman named Greta hides your only son and heir."

Moddan stiffened, the look of panic in his eyes. "Ye leave him alone!"

Thorfinn grinned. "Now, why would I do that?"

Moddan blurted out, "Rognvald had me set a large bounty on Orla's head. They willna stop coming for her unless she's dead. Spare my son, and I will do anything to stop them."

Dalziel entered the room carrying a sheet of vellum and a quill with inkpot. He placed them in front of Moddan and said, "You will write word for word what I tell you."

That night Moddan died a painful, gruesome death at Thorfinn's hand. A golden spear pierced his skull, dealing the death blow. His beaten body was wedged on a spike outside the castle gates for everyone to see.

Moddan's son slept soundly in his bed, unaware of how close to death he came that night.

A Father's Love

THORFINN SPENT SOME time thinking about Orla's safety. He had observed how protective Brodie was and how enamored Orla was with her husband. She had lost much in her young life. He did not want to take away any more of her happiness by separating her from Brodie.

The next morning Thorfinn met with his king.

"King Magnus, I wish to discuss the matter of my *dattar*."

"Whit, is it? I trust the annulment will soon be granted and she will come with me."

Thorfinn replied, "I have had a... change of heart."

"Tis not like you to change your mind on territorial matters."

"Aye, but dis is my *dattar*, more precious than territories."

Magnus sighed. "Very well, *whit* is it?"

"There is something better I can offer you," Thorfinn replied.

"Go on."

"Kalf Arnason, my fiancé's uncle, and your once most trusted advisor."

"Whit about him?"

"Ye said yerself last time we met, Kalf had a hand in your far's death."

"He did." Magnus clenched his jaw. "He killed my sire."

"Yet despite this, ye cannot kill him or exile him from royal court because you would lose the support of the Norwegian nobles. But the longer he remains in Norway, the greater risk he is to your crown."

Magnus nodded, "Tis true. He is a complication I have tried to rid myself of for months."

"Exile him to Orkney under my care. I will keep a close eye on him," Thorfinn said.

Magnus tilted his head and rubbed his chin. "Go on."

"If you exile him to Orkney, he is still on Norwegian soil, which will appease your nobles, but it removes his influence in court. He will also be close to Ingibiorg, who he treats as a *dattar*. The nobles cannot say you banished an old man to a place with no family if his niece is there."

Magnus's face broke out into an enormous smile. "Done!" he replied without hesitation. As much as Magnus craved Orla, his need to be rid of Kalf was far stronger.

They shook hands on it.

Thorfinn killed two birds with one stone. He knew Ingibiorg had a soft spot for her uncle, Kalf. This way, he would make her happy and give Orla the happiness she desired.

Thorfinn smiled to himself. Ever the shrewd politician, even in matters of the heart.

The Showdown

ORLA SAW THORFINN AND Magnus talking in the Upper Hall. It was time for her to put her foot down. She was done letting men decide her destiny. She had returned from the archery range and was in trews and tunic, still armed with bow, quiver, and daggers.

Orla stepped into the hall and addressed her father. "*Far!* I need a word, please."

"I am busy sweeting, but I will talk to you later." Thorfinn dismissed her.

Orla grabbed her bow, pulled out two arrows from the quiver strapped to her back, and nocked them in the taut bowstring. She aimed at Thorfinn and Magnus.

"Hey now! Whit is dis?" Magnus asked, moving out of her line of fire.

"*Dattar*, ye will not point that at me," Thorfinn grumbled.

"You will stop telling me what to do!" she yelled. "You will both listen to me or by the devil I will let my arrows fly."

"You dare threaten a jarl and a king?" Magnus asked, although he was smirking.

"Aye. When you're dead and buried, no one can tell whether your bones are that of a peasant or a king. We're all just bones in the dirt, none of the titles matter, so yes, I dare."

Both men contemplated her words and gave a begrudging nod.

"Well, my *dattar*, you have our undivided attention. What would you like to discuss?"

"You willna annul my marriage to Brodie, do you hear me? I love that big brute, and I cannot exist without him, so if you come between us, I will make sure you regret it," she hissed.

Thorfinn was proud of his daughter standing up to him. Pity, it was unnecessary, but he would play along.

Magnus was mesmerized and regretted his earlier agreement with Thorfinn. He thought Orla looked magnificent, especially when enraged.

"Wipe that look off your face, Magnus!" she bit out. "Get it into your head. I already have a man in my life. If you insist on taking me to Norway, I will cut off your manhood when you sleep and feed it to the fish." Orla was practically shouting now.

Magnus raised his hands palm up and said, "All right, you win. Because of your impassioned speech, I will withdraw my offer."

"You... you will?" Orla stammered in surprise.

"I will. I prefer my manhood where it is." Magnus grinned.

Orla redirected her arrows at Thorfinn. "And you, *Far*? Will you withdraw your request for annulment?"

"Aye, I will. You have made me see the foolishness of my ways, sweeting." Thorfinn looked as if he was trying not to laugh.

"Well, good. Good. I am pleased we had this talk and I hope in the future you two will allow women to get a word in sometimes." Orla un-nocked her arrows, turned on her heel, and marched out the door. *Humph, I showed them!* She muttered to herself.

Dolls

THE FOLLOWING DAY, King Magnus announced he and his men were leaving. Magnus requested a meeting with Orla to say goodbye. Brodie stood guard by the door just in case Magnus tried to kidnap his wife.

Magnus regretted they would probably never see each other again but wished Orla well. He also shared that he was leaving to retrieve his daughter, Ragnhild Magnusdatter. She was born out of wedlock, and he had secretly placed her in a convent away from Court. Their hasty departure meant he could not find a suitable Scottish gift for her. She had requested a doll, and alas, Magnus could not get hold of one.

"Wait there, Your Majesty, hold one moment."

Orla went to her chambers and retrieved the parcel Morag gave her with the doll inside.

She ran back to Magnus. "This is a gift from my family to your *dattar*."

When Magnus saw it, his face softened, and he smiled. "This is the most exquisite doll I have ever seen. She will treasure it. Thank you."

Orla just whispered, "You are welcome, Magnus."

Chapter 17 - Kiss of Death

A few nights later, the Great Hall was overflowing with courtiers and townsfolk to celebrate Macbeth's birthday. They had organized a large extravagant banquet for the occasion, and festivities were in full swing.

There was so much food. Orla found she was suddenly famished. The stress and threat of the past few weeks had affected her appetite and now she was happy to eat, drink and be merry. Orla was sitting close to Brodie and feeling happier than she had in a long time. Master Ajani sat across from her upon her insistence and her brother Kato sat beside her. He was speaking to her in both Amharic and English.

"How did you both learn Angles and Gaels?" Orla asked.

"Our *seti ayati*, or what you call *seanmathair*, invited many travelers and tutors who knew of such languages to teach us," Kato replied. "We each speak several languages which help us communicate with many foreigners."

Orla asked, "Really? These tutors traveled all the way to Abyssinia to teach you?"

"Well... Queen Gudit had them captured... but once they were there, they were *very* willing," Ajani replied.

Orla chuckled.

"What does Kato mean?" she asked.

"It means second born of twins."

"What name do they give to the firstborn of twins?"

"Zesiro. They can use it for boys and girls," Master Ajani replied.

Orla said the name out loud a few times. She liked it. "Did my ma name me Zesiro?"

"No, she named you Zala," Ajani replied.

Thorfinn's rumbling voice interrupted them, "Aye, Izara always said if she had a girl, she would call her Zala."

"*Mor* changed your name to Orla so as not to attract any more attention," Torstein said. He had joined their table and had been conversing with Master Ajani. Tales of a place called *Morocco* fascinated Torstein.

Orla was laughing at something her brother said when she took a sip of honey mead. It moved down her throat smoothly and made her feel warm and tingly inside. She sipped some more and felt suddenly drowsy. She could barely keep her eyes open, and then her breathing slowed. Everything slowed. The room spun. She tried to stand but could not. Her body and tongue felt heavy. She tugged on Brodie's sleeve. He turned just in time to see her falling.

The last thing Orla saw was Brodie's panicked face and his arms outstretched reaching for her as he roared. Then her eyelids closed, and all was darkness.

Orla drifted to a strange but ethereal place, and she saw her mother, Izara, smiling at her. Her mother said, "Sleep, Zala." And she did.

When Orla fell from her chair, pandemonium reigned. Her brother, Kato, was yelling for help, Brodie was beside himself. Dalziel bent next to her and felt for breathing and a pulse. They tried everything, but her face paled and her lips turned blue, her body still.

The healer was summoned, and fifteen minutes later, her verdict was death by poisoning.

"No!" Brodie shouted as he held Orla in his arms, weeping openly and rocking her body back and forth. He yelled for someone to get Amelia. But Amelia was miles away. When Dalziel confirmed Orla was no longer breathing, Brodie refused to believe she was gone. He kept telling everyone she had only fainted.

Several retainers had to pry him away, but he refused to leave her body. Fighting anyone who came near her. Eventually, they had no choice but to knock him out before he destroyed everything in the room.

MACBETH'S MEN SCOURED the castle trying to find signs of who did it, but they found no clue. Word soon spread that Orla, the Orphan of the MacGregor clan, had died.

Dalziel sent a missive to Beiste and Amelia that Orla had passed away. A grief-stricken Thorfinn decided to take her body for a proper Norse burial in Orkney, and Dalziel sent Brodie home with the MacGregor retainers since he had fallen seriously ill with a fever.

The MacGregor clan openly mourned, especially Amelia. She was inconsolable.

Brodie felt adrift. His universe tilted, and he sank into darkness and despair so bleak it consumed him.

Chapter 18 – Death Becomes Her

Brodie awoke in a dark room. He could hear voices and movement around the bed.

"Someone needs to tell him," Amelia whispered.

"Aye love, I will do it," Beiste replied.

He heard Amelia crying. But tell him what? *Where was Orla?* It was necessary for him to see Orla. Brodie had woken several times calling for Orla but felt fevered and clammy. As he slipped in and out of consciousness, he felt confused. Finally, he opened his eyes.

"Tell me what?" he asked.

Amelia and Beiste looked stricken.

He glanced around and winced in pain.

"Dinnae thrash about or you'll ruin your bandages."

"Where's Orla?" he asked again.

"Just rest. All will be well," Amelia replied.

"Why will no one tell me anything? I need to see Orla. Am I dying?"

"You're not dying. You took on fever from all your minor cuts after the siege at Dunsinane. You have been fighting an infection for three days," Beiste replied.

"Where am I?"

"Dalziel, had you moved back home so Amelia could tend to you."

"Then why are you all whispering? Just tell me where Orla is."

"Orla is gone," Beiste replied.

"Gone where?"

Amelia burst into tears. "Oh Brodie, Orla was poisoned and passed away."

There was silence.

"No! She just fainted, that was all she just fainted. Brother?" Brodie looked at Beiste to confirm, but Beiste just shook his head. He saw Amelia with tears streaming down her face and reality hit.

"Brodie, I am so sorry," Amelia choked out.

"Tell me this cannot be true!" He clutched Beiste's arm.

"She is dead. Thorfinn took her body to Orkney for a proper burial."

"No, no, it cannot be. She was alive, she was still breathing, she just fainted!" Brodie wept. He tried to sit up but collapsed onto the bed, inconsolable.

"There was nothing we could do," Beiste said.

"Go away!" he yelled.

"Brodie—" Amelia was about to say more.

"Mistress please, just leave me alone."

Brodie stared at the walls, tears streaming down his face. It was as if his entire life had ended in those words. *Orla is gone.*

His woman. His love. Gone. And he did not know how he would ever survive. He could battle with sword and axe, he could take on fifty men, but this inextricable grief, the emptiness within him, could not be assuaged. It physically hurt to breathe.

"My sweet huntress... my sweet huntress," he whispered over and over into nothingness.

Two Weeks Later

AMELIA SAID, "HUSBAND, I am so worried. Brodie has stopped eating altogether. He willna even see Iona or Colban. He willna talk to his men. It's like he's not there."

"We must give him more time, Amie. That's all he needs."

Brodie sat in his room staring out the window and, like every day since he learned of Orla's death, he opened the stopper of his whiskey bottle and drank. He needed to numb the pain and maybe, just maybe, he would get through another day without her.

The Murrays

DALZIEL ARRIVED WITH a message. "I have tried to make peace where I can, but this came today from Macbeth."

Beiste reached out taking the parchment. After reading it, he said, "Damn it to hell! This will destroy Brodie."

"Why, what is it?" Amelia asked.

"Tis from the Murrays. The chieftain's daughter is five months pregnant."

"So?" Amelia looked confused.

"She claims Brodie is the da and they're demanding a wedding."

"No, that cannot be. Beiste, he has suffered enough. Please do something," Amelia pleaded.

"The Murrays petitioned the king and seeing as Brodie is now a widower, Macbeth conceded the marriage is to go-ahead by the end of the sennight, to keep the peace."

"What if we refuse? I mean, we need proof. Surely this woman could be lying," Amelia asked.

"We all ken Brodie's reputation with the lassies, twill be difficult to dispute, and we cannot openly defy the king," Dalziel replied.

"Then one of you better tell him because there is no way I can bear to see any more heartbreak in that poor man's eyes," Amelia replied.

"SHE SAYS I DID WHAT?" Brodie shouted in disbelief.

"The Murray lass is claiming the bairn is yours and her da has received Macbeth's decree that you wed her within the sennight," Dalziel replied.

'Then she is a liar! I didn't bed her!"

"The chieftain claims it was a drunken night when you were last with the guardsman at Murray keep. You seduced his daughter and left the next morning."

Brodie cast his mind back. He remembered visiting, but he did not imbibe. He distinctly slept alone. "She is five months along?"

"Aye."

"Then it cannot be me. I have bedded no lass other than Orla this past year. She is lying!"

"Brodie, it matters not anymore. Tis Macbeth's decision," Dalziel replied.

"And I'm telling you, I didn't bed any wench in the last year for her to be expecting my bairn."

"C'mon Brodie, are you certain? We all ken how you love to swive—"

"Stop right there, Dalziel. I will say it again, I have bedded no woman in the past year. How could I? Orla was all I could think about." Brodie looked outraged.

"Then we have a problem. Macbeth has decreed it and the Murrays are out for blood."

"Well, she's a liar and I'll be damned if I marry a lying wench who is trying to palm off a bastard child onto me."

Beiste rubbed his forehead. "Brodie, I am sorry, but this marriage must go ahead. Tis crucial for all clans involved, we dinnae defy Macbeth. But trust me, we will seek an annulment once we find out the truth."

Second Marriage

IT WAS THE MORNING of Brodie's second marriage and only three and a half weeks after his wife's death. Brodie was resigned to his fate. It seemed as if the universe conspired against him to ensure he was as miserable today as he was the day Orla died.

Brodie bathed and dressed, and he even ate some food. Only because Amelia would not leave him alone with her incessant nagging. The woman was infuriating. How Beiste put up with her, he would never understand.

Now that he looked half decent, he downed four cups of whiskey to numb the pain. He could not care less what his new bride thought of him because he had no intention of touching her. There was already a babe in her belly. No one expected the marriage to be consummated and he sure as hell could not stomach making love to any other woman.

As there was still time before the ceremony, Brodie lay back on his bed, fully clothed, and just stared at the ceiling. He did not care that he would rumple his clothes, which Amelia had painstakingly prepared for him, or that his hair now looked disheveled. Brodie did not care at all.

He wondered, not for the first time, if this was how his father felt after Brodie's ma left him. *Is that why his da never stopped drinking?* Brodie still could not understand how his da became so violent. Even drunk, Brodie did not feel a need to hit anyone. He just wanted to lie down and die.

He must have fallen asleep because Brodie was startled awake by the sight of Morag, her white eyes and grey hair, leaning over him.

"Morag, you scared me. What do you want?"

"Och, look at ye now, feeling sorry for yerself. Tis, time. Get up Brodie, yer new bride is here, and she is a right bonnie lass."

"I dinnae care, Morag, I will never love her or even like her."

"Brodie, I miss Orla too, but she is gone. Ye have to accept that."

Brodie rolled out of bed and stood. "Dinnae say that. I will never accept it. Never!"

Beiste entered the room. "Brodie, calm. Let us go now."

Brodie nodded and walked out the door. He may as well be marching to his death. He just hoped the ceremony was quick so he could drown his sorrows in wedding wine.

"I want you to ken Beiste. I do this for the clan. But once tis done, I expect you all to leave me be."

"Aye we will Brodie," Beiste replied.

BRODIE WALKED INTO the chapel and straight to the front of the altar. He did not greet anyone. He wanted this blasted day over.

"At least try to look amenable to your bride-to-be," Dalziel said as he came to stand beside Brodie.

"I dinnae care to be amenable to that deceitful wench."

"Brodie, you're making this so much more difficult than it needs to be," Dalziel said.

"Does no one care that I lost the love of my life? Does no one care that she's not yet cold in the grave and now I'm being forced to wed some stranger based on a falsehood?" He gritted his teeth.

"Aye, I ken it cannot be easy for you, Brodie, but trust me. All will be well."

"How the hell do you ken that, Dalziel? Nothing will *ever* be well again. Not for me."

The Wedding March

THE MUSICIAN PLAYED a slow tune as a hush came over the crowd.

Brodie was oblivious. He just stared straight ahead at the chapel windows and blocked everything else out of his mind. Brodie could hear people milling about even so, he refused to look anywhere but straight ahead. Eventually, he heard people taking their seats and the rustling of material and slight footsteps.

He had no intention of greeting his bride. She could rot in hell for all he cared. He kept a scowl on his face. Brodie could see from the side of his eye the shape of a woman in a heavy veil, slowly making her way down the aisle, but he did not bother to pay any attention. No doubt she was concealing her baby bump with all that frippery. He just clenched his jaw.

Brodie turned to look at Dalziel, who just shrugged his shoulders. He looked to his right side and saw the King and Queen with Beiste, Amelia and the bairns, Jonet, Sorcha, and Morag. He also noticed golden hair and wondered what the hell Torstein was doing there. Then he saw Jarl Thorfinn and Ajani and Kato. What he did *not* see was a single member of the Murray clan.

Just who the hell was he marrying?

He whirled back to the front and noticed his bride had just reached the altar beside him.

"Good lord, you smell like a brewery, Brodie Fletcher! What the hell have you been drinking?"

Brodie froze. He knew that voice. He had dreamed of that voice a thousand times. He turned to look at his bride for the first time and, without warning; he ripped off her veil and stopped breathing.

"Orla?" he asked in disbelief.

She scowled at him. "Brodie Fletcher, it took me an age to get my hair done and now you've gone and ruin—"

Before she could finish, Brodie pulled her into his arms, and his lips came crashing down on hers. Orla flung her arms around his shoulders and returned the kiss with ardor.

"Och, stop that now, no groping in a church!" Thorfinn growled.

Brodie broke the kiss and began caressing Orla's face and her hair, her arms. "But how? Are you real? Am I dreaming?"

"I am real, Brodie and you are very much awake," Orla whispered.

They gazed at one another with tears shimmering in their eyes.

Brodie suddenly felt weak, as if he were going to fall. He paused for a moment and glanced at the crowd. Brodie looked at Abbot Hendry, Beiste, and Amelia. The three of them held shocked expressions. Jonet and Sorcha also had their mouths wide open.

Brodie glanced at Dalziel and noticed the man was *not* the least bit surprised. Then Brodie saw red. He released Orla, drew back his arm, and punched Dalziel right in the face. "What the devil did you do?" he roared as he leapt on Dalziel to pummel him some more. The two men tumbled to the ground.

"This is the house of God. There will be no violence in here!" Abbot Hendry was shouting and trying to regain control.

Dalziel dodged the blows as best he could until Beiste and Torstein restrained Brodie and pulled him off Dalziel.

"You son of a bitch! Do you ken the hell I've been living through?" he shouted at Dalziel.

"Aye, I deserved that." Dalziel rubbed his sore jaw. "I'm sorry, but I'll explain all of it later. Right now, you both need to get married again before everyone changes their mind."

"You'll keep." Brodie glared at Dalziel before turning back to Orla and asking, "Why?"

Orla replied with pure love shining in her eyes, "Twas out of my hands, Brodie. Even I did not ken the plan until—"

Brodie gazed at her and knew that whatever the reason, she was his and he would never squander a single moment with her again. He abruptly said, "I dinnae care. We will talk later." He pulled Orla into his side and ordered the abbot to, "Get on with it!"

At the end of the ceremony, and as the parchment of marriage would attest, Brodie Fletcher was officially married to *Zala Thorfinnsdottir.*

⚜

THERE WAS A SMALL WEDDING feast afterward, but Brodie was not having a bar of it. He grabbed Orla's hand and stormed past everyone.

"Brodie, where are you going?" Amelia yelled.

He turned to the room and declared, "I am going to bed my new wife, Zala, and make sure tis legal. Do what you like."

He could hear chuckles and guffaws, and he did not care.

Brodie carried his bride up the stairs. When they reached his room (which he was glad someone had cleaned in his absence) he slammed the door shut with his foot, put Orla on her feet, and just stared at her. His heart was full to overflowing, his cock was hard as iron, and he looked like a wild animal starved of affection for far too long.

Orla stared at her lover, her nipples hard, her core wet with anticipation, and she was panting.

Then, as fast as lightning, they attacked one another with frantic need.

Brodie tore the clothes from her body, grabbed the back of her neck, and kissed her hard as Orla pulled off his plaid and tore his shirt open. They sucked, bit, and licked wherever they found exposed skin. Orla wrapped her arms around his neck to deepen the kiss.

Orla moaned when Brodie lifted her up so she could straddle his hips.

"Wrap your legs around me. I'm going to take you standing," he growled.

"Aye," Orla gasped as she ground her core against his length and bit his neck.

Brodie pushed her back against the wall and suckled her nipples.

"I cannot hold out much longer, love," he said.

"Shut up and do it. I'm tired of wait—"

Before Orla could finish her line, Brodie jerked his hips and thrust his full length inside her. She threw her head back and moaned. She had forgotten how large he was.

Brodie groaned at how tight his wife felt. He placed his forehead against hers, then pounded her against the wall with deep thrusts. The sensation was so overwhelming Orla screamed as she met his deep thrusts in return, biting and licking, gripping his shoulders, and hanging on. Brodie took her with such force the wall shook as he moved inside her.

After what felt like an eternity, he hit her pleasure spot and she came instantly. Her channel spasmed so hard around Brodie's length it triggered his climax. He groaned and jerked several times inside her before he flooded her with the warmth of his release. Her inner walls shuddered as she moaned in pleasure.

Orla felt euphoric, sated, and complete. She finally understood firsthand how such an activity could be accomplished against the wall.

Brodie kissed her softly. His eyes awash with tears, he said, "I've missed you, Zala Fletcher."

Orla burst into tears and replied, "I've missed you too, my love."

SOMETIME LATER, WHEN they had recovered from their emotional fueled coupling, while they were dressing to re-join the wedding festivities, Brodie said, "Tis glad I am I dinnae have to wed a woman with a bairn already inside of her."

Orla took a deep breath and replied, "Well, husband, there may be a slight problem with that."

"What do you mean?"

Zala took Brodie's hand and gently placed it on her belly.

"You jest?" Brodie said in awe.

She shook her head. "You're going to be a da, Brodie."

Brodie's face split into a wide grin, and before she could say anything else, he picked her up and planted another searing kiss on her lips.

Then he stilled.

"What's wrong, Brodie?"

"Did I hurt you or the bairn just now against the wall? Was I too rough?"

"Tis fine, husband, we are fine."

Brodie put her down and started pacing while running his hands through his hair. "Tis not fine, Zala. Tis dangerous. From now on, there is to be no coupling between us."

"Excuse me?" she raised a brow. She noticed how Brodie only called her Zala now, and she liked it.

"Aye, you heard me, you saucy vixen. I cannot be gentle where you are concerned, so you will need to not attack me."

"Attack you?"

"Aye, you need to stop this obsession you have with my braw body. Tis not safe for our bairn."

"My obsession? You're the one who tore off my clothes!"

"Tis precisely my point. From now on you will wear many layers of clothing to bed so we cannot couple in haste."

"Mark my words husband, there is no way I am going to not ride your glorious manhood every chance I get, so be warned."

Orla opened the door and was about to storm down the stairs when Brodie picked her up and carried her. She had no choice but to wind her arms about his neck as he walked them downstairs.

"What are you doing?" Orla asked.

"You are not to walk or run or even skip downstairs. You could fall and hurt yourself and our bairn."

"Brodie Fletcher, you cannot stop me from walking!"

"I can and I will. Come to think of it, you may not ride a horse or go outdoors either."

"Then how will I move around the Keep?"

"I will carry you wherever you need to go," he replied in all seriousness.

"No, you willna carry me about like a bairn."

"We'll see," he said in a smug voice.

"Brodie Fletcher, you are the most irritating man I have ever met," Orla huffed.

Brodie chuckled. Gads how he had missed his wife and now the sexy minx was back.

Not only had his lover and soul mate returned to him, but they also had a babe on the way.

Plans Revealed

THAT NIGHT, DALZIEL explained to the MacGregors and Brodie why they had to fake Orla's death. It was because the bounty Moddan set on her head was too high. Men would keep coming after Orla unless Thorfinn formally recognized her as his daughter and under his protection.

Thorfinn could not formally recognize his illegitimate children until he wed Ingibiorg. Magnus placed that condition on Thorfinn to ensure he kept his agreement to exile Ingibiorg's uncle Kalf at Orkney.

Naturally, it took some time to convince Ingibiorg to marry in haste. In the meantime, they needed an interim plan.

Dalziel said, "Twas Moddan, who gave me the idea. He told me men would keep coming after Orla *unless she was dead*. So, I made the arrangements. Only Macbeth, Thorfinn and Ajani kenned the plan."

"Why didn't you tell us?" Beiste asked. "The anguish we went through was terrible."

"It had to look real. Only raw emotion and open grieving would ensure the word spread. Even Orla was not aware of what I had planned. I slipped her a draught, to slow her breathing down but not kill her. I needed as many public witnesses to her death as possible."

"Is she safe now?" Amelia asked.

"Aye, the plan was only to buy us enough time until Thorfinn could enact his part. Rognvald is oblivious to the truth."

"So, what happens now?" Beiste asked.

"There is one more thing left to do."

"What's that?" Brodie asked.

"You and Zala need to go to Orkney."

Chapter 19 – The Reckoning

Brusi's Island, Shetland

Rognvald Brusisson received two missives. He opened the first one and saw it contained Moddan's handwriting. It was dated to the previous month. He settled in and smiled the more he read until he was virtually dancing around his chambers. It was the news he had waited to hear. Thorfinn and Izara's daughter was dead. Thorfinn never knew of her existence and was returning to his seat as Mormaer of Caithness, where he would share the rule of Orkneys.

The second missive was from Thorfinn, notifying Rognvald he was returning home and invited Rognvald to a celebratory feast in Kirkwall.

Kirkwall, Orkney Isles

ROGNVALD WALKED WITH a spring in his step as he ascended the steps to the jarl's stronghold. The long-absent Thorfinn 'the Mighty' had finally returned to settle in Orkney and rumor was he was in a festive mood. Thorfinn often held large celebratory feasts lasting several days.

Rognvald breathed a sigh of relief, knowing that he had dodged a fire arrow, and congratulated himself on tying up loose ends before the jarl arrived.

He thought it strange Moddan had yet to return from Dunsinane, but it was possible the man had other matters to attend to. Rognvald hoped that now the air was clear between them. He and Thorfinn could begin a new peaceful era between the earls of Orkney. Now that it was just Thorfinn and Rognvald left of the Sigurdsson line, he had hoped Thorfinn would look upon him as a son and not just a nephew.

He was ushered to the high table of the Great Hall, which was brimming with people. Thorfinn greeted him.

"Come nephew, tis wonderful to see you again." Thorfinn hugged him then directed him to his seat.

"Welcome home, Uncle, I trust your raiding was successful."

"Aye, it wis. But now, I have a mind to settle doon. Allow me to introduce my new wife, Ingibiorg." Thorfinn ushered a beautiful woman forward, and she was genteel, with blue eyes and golden locks. She was also softly spoken.

Rognvald made the polite greetings, then resumed his seat. He was surprised first that Thorfinn was married, but also how Thorfinn's face softened when he gazed at his wife. Rognvald watched Thorfinn fuss over Ingibiorg. He even pulled her chair closer to his and held her hand.

A light repast was served as they spoke for some time about matters regarding the Isles. Rognvald noticed several empty seats at the High table. He wondered who the other guests were when the doors to the hall opened. A hush fell over the crowd as all conversation and music ceased.

Rognvald turned to see a tall man with light brown skin and strange robes walking into the hall. Behind walked an older man with darker skin and similar robes. On either side of his garments hung a scabbard and a curved sword.

There was something familiar about the younger man. The way he strode into the room and his striking brown eyes. Rognvald knew those eyes well. He turned to look at Thorfinn and saw a replica pair staring back at him.

His heart beat faster as he tried to piece together what he suspected but could not accept as feasible.

Thorfinn stood and spoke in a booming voice, "Allow me to introduce my firstborn son, Kato Thorfinnsson of the Royal House of *Habesha* and his guardsman, Master Ajani Nuru."

Murmurings started from the crowd as people stared, mesmerized by the strange turn of events.

"Tis fortunate for you. He does not want our territory. He has his own kingdom many miles away," Thorfinn quietly said to Rognvald.

Prince Kato took his place at the high table, but Ajani preferred to stand guard along the wall.

"But how?"

"Moddan may have killed my beloved Izara, but he underestimated one thing: a mother's protective instincts for her children."

Kato said, "She saved her babies and gave her life for them."

Rognvald was feeling uncomfortable. The crowd hushed and Rognvald looked beyond Thorfinn to see another woman emerge from the side chamber.

He gasped, "No, it cannot be?"

Thorfinn once again addressed the crowd. "May I present Kato's twin sister, Zala Thorfinnsdottir. She is under my protection."

"Fletcher, her last name is Fletcher," Brodie grumbled as he followed behind Orla, now formally referred to as Zala.

Thorfinn just rolled his eyes.

An attendant brought forth Thorfinn's golden spear. Thorfinn held it, then addressed the assembly.

"Heed my words!" he roared. "Anyone who harms my offspring will die by my hand and I will paint the sea red with the blood of their descendants!" Thorfinn did a war cry and hurled his golden spear across the hall, so it lodged in the main door. "Spread my words far and wide lest my golden spear comes for you in the night!"

After his words, the crowd got to their feet. A roaring chant erupted as they banged their feet on the wooden floorboards and pounded their cups on the tables.

Thorfinn knew by nightfall the following day, his message would have spread across most of *Alba* and the *Isles*. When he sat back down, the musicians resumed playing as platters of decadent food and jugs of ale flowed freely. The festivities had well and truly begun.

Hagan, Runa, Torstein, and his men were also present at the feast. Thorfinn gifted them with land and riches to thank them for protecting his twins. To Torstein, he gifted a *snekkja* warship of his own. Thorfinn also arranged a large sum of coins to be gifted to Beiste and to Morag to thank the clan for sheltering his daughter. Thorfinn forbade Norse raiders from Orkney and Shetland to raid the MacGregor's land.

As for his son, Kato, and Master Ajani, Thorfinn had already decided he would transport them back to the *Port of Zeila* himself. There was much Thorfinn wanted to learn about alternative trade routes and continents. He also had restitution to pay to an Abyssinian queen.

Rognvald could not stop perspiring. It was the most uncomfortable feast he had ever attended. But he knew his days were numbered and that King Magnus, his once closest ally, had abandoned him. He knew this because in all the missives he had received from Magnus, the king never mentioned that Orla had been at Macbeth's castle with Thorfinn.

Late into the night, when people were well into their cups, Thorfinn approached Rognvald and said, "Moddan is dead, and so are all your followers. Enjoy your seat in *Shetland* for now. But ken this, nephew, by the time my new wife gives me a son, your reign will be over."

Rognvald paled in his seat. Thorfinn just tapped him twice on the shoulder and walked away.

Ring of Brodgar, Stenness, Orkney Isles

IT WAS A COOL AUTUMN day. The sun was shining its glorious rays upon a breathtaking landscape.

Zala and Brodie walked in silence, hand in hand among the stone circle, just enjoying the peaceful surroundings and each other. Zala felt a deep connection to the Orkneys. It was in her blood. They had spent two weeks enjoying the scenery and the coastal air and were traveling home the following day.

In the time they had spent in Orkney, she knew Ingibiorg better and liked the woman. Thorfinn had warmed to Brodie, and he had taken him on short sailing trips to the outer isles. Thorfinn even had a square head axe with an Orkney crest made especially for Brodie. Brodie begrudgingly admitted that Thorfinn was an outstanding fighter, despite being an old decrepit man.

Zala also spent a great deal of time with her twin brother Kato and Master Ajani. They had given her a 'shotel' sword of her own, which she carried everywhere in a specially made leather scabbard. It had been forged in an ancient place called *Eritrea*, and Orla carried it with pride. She still could not believe they were royalty and had much to learn about the new worlds opened up to her.

She and Brodie had decided not to travel to the *Port of Zeila* with them. Now that Zala was with child, she wanted only to be at home with her husband in their own house. Instead, she had prepared several missives for her grandmother the Queen. Zala wanted her to know she was happy and safe, and someday she would make the long journey with her family.

Epilogue

1044 Fletcher House, Scotland

"Thorfinn Kato Fletcher, you put that axe down now!" Zala was glaring at her son with her hands on her hips. He was a miniature version of his father, baby battle axe included.

"Iza hit me wif awow," he bellowed, speaking almost unintelligibly as Zala tried to decipher his meaning.

"I din hit ye!" screamed his twin sister.

"Izara Amelia Fletcher, did you hit your brother with an arrow?" Zala scowled at her.

"No, I missed," her daughter replied.

"What is all this shouting? Can't a man get any sleep in his own house?" Brodie joined the chaos. He looked disheveled, red-rimmed eyes shirtless and wearing only his plaid. Zala thought her husband was the most handsome man in the Highlands, especially when bare-chested.

Brodie walked straight over to his daughter and removed the bow and arrow she was wielding. "You willna have these again until you learn to take care."

Then he stormed over to his son and took the battle axe away from him. "And you'll not have this again until you can wield it wisely."

He placed the weapons on top of a shelf, then bent to the same level as his children and gathered them together. "These weapons are to be used to protect one another. Never use them on each other, understand?"

Both children nodded, then flung themselves at their father, who gave them a bear hug. Brodie then picked them up, one in each arm. "Tis time for breakfast."

Brodie carried them to the kitchens and placed them at the table as Cook started fussing over them. He then returned to Zala, and kissed her cheek, whispering in her ear, "I've arranged for Amelia to take the bairns for the day after they break their fast."

"Why?" she asked.

"So, we can get busy making some more." He winked at her.

"And what game do you suggest we play this time, Brodie Fletcher?" Zala asked in a sultry voice.

"I was thinking we could play the *Bear* eats the *Huntress* and then the *Huntress* rides the *Bear*."

An hour and a half later, they played many games for the rest of the day until they collapsed, sated, in each other's arms.

Dalziel

DALZIEL WATCHED THE spectacle before him. It was May Day celebrations, and happy families surrounded him. The clan gathered around the loch with long trestle tables teeming with platters of food and beverages as people celebrated the first day of Spring. There was dancing and singing and laughter. The clan had survived another harsh winter and were now enjoying the fruits of spring.

Dalziel was glad that his two brothers in arms had found the love and fulfillment they deserved with women worthy of their love.

Although it reminded him of how solitary his life had become of late. In his line of work, he could not afford to get attached to any woman beyond physical need. He thought about the mission he had for the king and clenched his jaw. He gripped his cup of cider as he stared out into the distance.

"Why so broody? Tis a celebration to be enjoyed," Sorcha said.

"If only," Dalziel replied and smiled at her.

A messenger interrupted them with a missive. Dalziel studied the parchment. It had come from his trusted contact Mr. Arrowsmith, another of Macbeth's spies who moonlighted as a bowyer in Northumbria.

Dalziel clenched his jaw when he read, "Lady Clarissa seen in the company of an unknown French man."

"What is it?" Beiste asked, carrying his two-month-old son, Dalziel Brodie MacGregor.

"I need to leave now," Dalziel replied.

"You cannot leave before they light the bonfire," Amelia said. Disgruntled that a member of the family was leaving the festivities so soon.

"There is trouble brewing at my holdings in *Anglia*."

"What kind of trouble? Do you need me to come with you?" Brodie piped in holding a sleeping Izara.

"No, tis more of a delicate matter."

"How so?" Zala asked, concern marring her facial expression as she tried to stop little Thorfinn from poking his finger in all the cakes.

"Tis my wife," Dalziel replied.

They all looked surprised. "You have a wife?" they cried in unison.

"Och ye sly fox." Morag chuckled.

"How could you not tell us you have a wife?" Jonet looked most displeased.

"Aye, we should meet her now that she is family," Sorcha said.

"Tis in name only. We were pledged last summer."

They were all quiet, not knowing what to say in response to his statement. They knew Dalziel held a lot of secrets, but this was by far the biggest one.

"Is she well?" Amelia asked whilst monitoring Colban and Iona dancing around the maypole with other children.

"Aye, she is well, but I need to remind her who she belongs to," Dalziel growled.

1044 Dalziel's Estate, Northumbria

DALZIEL ARRIVED CLOSE to midnight. He had ridden hard through thundering rain all the way from Scotland.

He arrived unannounced. The element of surprise was always a good way to discover what was really going on. The way the servants scurried around like frightened mice at his appearance made him glad he did.

He stormed inside the main foyer and was accosted by his steward, Mr. Bell, and his housekeeper, Mrs. Armstrong.

"My Lord! We were not expecting you tonight. Is everything all right?" Mrs. Armstrong asked as Mr. Bell took his sodden coat and handed him a towel to dry his hair.

"Aye, I am sorry I did not message ahead, but some urgent matters had me returning early. Where is Lady Clarissa?" Dalziel asked calmly.

"She is..." Mr. Bell looked at Mrs. Armstrong. They looked nervous.

"Not in, my lord," Mrs. Armstrong replied.

"What do you mean she is not in? Tis almost midnight," Dalziel asked.

He turned to Mr. Bell, awaiting a response. He saw two maids and three male servants in the background hovering.

"Lady Clarissa is attending a gathering," Mr. Bell stated.

"Which one? I ken no such events happening tonight," Dalziel asked, sounding calm, although inside he was feeling anything but calm.

Dalziel could see the servants were uncomfortable. But he had done his research beforehand and there were no gatherings happening within the shire that would warrant his wife being out in this inclement weather.

Mr. Bell cast a nervous glance at Mrs. Armstrong, who subtly shrugged her shoulders. Both were seemingly at a loss for words.

Dalziel knew they were hiding something. Even the maids were complicit. If he found out his wife was cuckolding him, he would lose his mind. Without another word, he walked up the flight of stairs and began opening every single door, thinking he may find her with a lover. The more he searched, the angrier he became, which was so out of character for him. He never allowed anger or any emotion to dictate his behavior.

Dalziel was standing on the landing above the main entrance when the main doors flew open and a figure came marching in with confident strides. Then he heard her voice. Dalziel stilled and looked down at the grand entranceway.

"Bugger me, Cecil," she said, taking off her coat. "The weather is cold out. Damn near froze my tits off! But look…" She fished something out of her pocket and gave it to Mrs. Armstrong. "I won it back! All right, I admit I cheated, but they stole it, so in this case two wrongs make a right."

Dalziel stared at the woman in the moon's light, and it was as if he was staring down at a stranger. She had his wife's voice, but that was where the resemblance ended.

Underneath the coat, she wore men's clothes. Trews, shirt, cap, and flat boots. If anyone was looking from afar, they would think she was a lad.

A riot of auburn hair spilled out when she pulled off the cap. She was wet, and her clothes clung to every aspect of her body. She kept talking, wringing out her hair as the servants handed her towels. All subtly gesturing for Clarissa to be quiet.

Dalziel wondered who this strange woman was who could garner the loyalty of his staff? What was this manner of dress and speech? This was not the prim, dull wallflower he had married. That female was a paragon of propriety and boring pursuits and rarely spoke a word... but this... this woman was something else entirely.

Mr. Bell cleared his throat, trying to give Clarissa warning signals, but she carried on oblivious. "Oh, before I forget, I've sent word that no one heads to the Cove tonight. Tis especially dangerous where they've stored the—."

"Mistress! We have company," Mrs. Armstrong practically scream-shouted over her.

Clarissa stopped drying her hair and asked, "At this hour? Who is it?"

Dalziel moved down the stairs, trying to keep his fury in check. She must have sensed his approach because she spun around in shock and gasped when she saw him.

Dalziel took in her lush, wet figure and her flushed face as he stalked towards her. The wolf within him unleashed with a feral need to claim.

When he was standing directly in front of her, he stared into her emerald eyes and in a lethal voice said, "Hello, Wife. Where the hell have you been?"

The End

Dalziel & Clarissa's story is up next...
https://elinaemerald.com/books
Sign up for Elina's Newsletter & Free Story
https://dl.bookfunnel.com/aiq0ubhpx6
Buy Direct & Save
https://payhip.com/elinaemerald

Notes

Orla was initially a minor character in Book 1. However, as I am learning with my writing process, the characters determine their significance in my books, not me. By the time I was midway through writing the first book, Orla had risen from a minor character to someone worthy of her own story.

Because I had already mentioned she was mixed raced with darker skin, I had locked myself into a worldwide medieval tour of epic proportions. The question I started with was how did a woman of color end up in the Scottish Highlands during the reign of the Red King?

For me, the logical place to begin was the Orkney Isles, which were annexed by Norway, and became a key trading point along the Viking western route during medieval times. This led me to one of the greatest and most powerful Jarls of Orkney, Thorfinn Sigurdsson (from the Orkneyinga Saga which outlines the history of the earls of Orkncy) also known as 'Thorfinn the Mighty' and 'Thorfinn the Black.'

They described him as a big, dark, brutish and extremely 'ugly' man. I fell in love instantly because he reminded me of the complex Edward Rochester in Bronte's Jane Eyre. My imagination soared, and knowing nothing else about him, I decided he was Orla's father and that was it.

The struggle I had with the Orkney Isles and Shetland and Norway was in trying to capture the dialect. Norn language was spoken in the Orkneys during this period, and it was difficult.

Next, I needed to figure out who Orla's mother was and how she ended up with Orla's father and as I traced possible Viking routes...

before I knew it; I had stumbled upon the most amazing history about medieval Warrior Queens from Cush and Abyssinia. I'm talking really bad-ass women who not only ruled sovereign over vast expansive regions, but they also destroyed empires twice their size and kept enemies at bay with sheer military might and strategy. They were feared and revered.

Queen Yodit Gudit is just one notable historical figure reigning sovereign over a region that covered Abyssinia to Yemnat (Ethiopia to Yemeni). There is a lot of contention around whether she really was a rebel queen or a legitimate successor to the throne. She is a controversial figure. One interesting thing about her is she apparently single-handedly destroyed the Aksumite (Axumite) Empire (not sure if that was a good thing). Aksum is an empire we know very little about today because there are not enough historical records left from that era except some highly advanced coins (plausible conclusion, Gudit destroyed everything on her warpath).

However, one notable historical figure from Aksum is The Queen of Sheba mentioned in 1 Kings of the Old Testament of the Bible. She sought the wisdom of King Solomon, and he gave her everything she wanted in return. Rumor has it they had a son together, and the Ark of the Covenant (a chest containing the Ten Commandments) is hidden in the city of Aksum. In the book of Philippians in the New Testament of the Bible, there is mention of an Ethiopian eunuch who served as treasurer to an Ethiopian Queen. But I digress. The point is you can find a lot of ancient references and scholarly articles on warrior queens from these regions.

What I found interesting from a sociological perspective is what little exposure Black History receives when we talk about medieval times. It is not uncommon because the Middle Ages are defined in terms of European History. However, we need to remember great empires existed outside Great Britain and Europe during this period. This compelled me to write a bit of this history into Book 2. Not because I'm on some crusade to educate the masses, or romanticize my ideal medieval world, it's because it's part of medieval history.

Now, I feel the need to talk about Rognvald Brusisson and his father, Brusi Sigurdsson, Thorfinn's half-brother. They were, by most accounts, great men. Brusi was a peacemaker and popular and well-liked, and he had a kind disposition. He also took care of Orkney and Shetland Isles often because Thorfinn was away on raids across Alba. In a nutshell, Thorfinn kills Brusi, his half-brother, and Rognvald, his nephew over territory and other points of contention. Thorfinn also had two sons with Ingibiorg who took over as earls of Orkney. I just want to mention in these notes I think Brusi and his son Rognvald got the short end of the stick. They should have been left in peace to rule their territories, but in the end, they were outplayed by a master strategist.

Right, I think that's enough history for one sitting. I need to save something for the next book.

Thanks again for reading.

Elina x

Did you love *Handfasted to the Bear*? Then you should read *Pledged to the Wolf* by Elina Emerald!

Dalziel 'the Wolf' Robertson is an enigma with many secrets. Part English and part Scots, he is silent, calculating, and deadly. The traits one needs to be the Red King's assassin (Book 2). Estranged from his mother's side, he abhors all things English, and with the exception of his inner circle of brothers and the occasional mistress, he is content to live a reclusive life. That is until he finds himself pledged to an English wallflower with a notorious reputation for being extremely dull. For some reason, she intrigues him and threatens his resolve.Among the gentry, Clarissa Harcourt is considered to be a quiet, proper, boring wallflower. Finding herself in impoverished circumstances, she agrees to wed an unknown Scottish Highlander for a year and a day. It will be

---

1. https://books2read.com/u/4XLXwa
2. https://books2read.com/u/4XLXwa

a marriage of convenience, enabling her to maintain her ruse because Clarissa has secrets of her own. Secrets that will place her life and heart at risk.Warning: Brawny alpha males ahead and historical inaccuracies. Not suitable for readers under 18. It contains mature content.

Read more at https://elinaemerald.com/books.

About the Author

Elina Emerald is a South Pacific-born Australian author who grew up in *Wiradjuri* and *Yuin* country.

A lawyer and research sociologist by trade, she spent several years songwriting and touring with an indie band. Elina developed a penchant for castles, old ruins, and medieval world history in her travels worldwide. She now writes Romantic Suspense books in different subgenres.

Read more at https://elinaemerald.com/.

CPSIA information can be obtained
at www.ICGtesting.com
Printed in the USA
LVHW041041120723
752272LV00005B/107